Swimming Naked

STACY SIMS

Swimming Naked

VIKING

VIKING

Published by the Penguin Group

Penguin Group (USA) Inc., 375 Hudson Street, New York, New York, 10014, U.S.A.

Penguin Books Ltd, 80 Strand, London WC2R 0RL, England

Penguin Books Australia Ltd, 250 Camberwell Road, Camberwell,
    Victoria 3124, Australia

Penguin Books Canada Ltd, 10 Alcorn Avenue, Toronto, Ontario, Canada M4V 3B2

Penguin Books India (P) Ltd, 11 Community Centre, Panchsheel Park,
    New Dehli – 110 017, India

Penguin Books (N.Z.) Ltd, Cnr Rosedale and Airborne Roads, Albany,
    Auckland, New Zealand

Penguin Books (South Africa) (Pty) Ltd, 24 Sturdee Avenue,
    Rosebank, Johannesburg 2196, South Africa

Penguin Books Ltd, Registered Offices:
80 Strand, London WC2R 0RL, England

First published in 2004 by Viking Penguin,
a member of Penguin Group (USA) Inc.

10 9 8 7 6 5 4 3 2 1

Grateful acknowledgment is made for permission to reprint excerpts from the following copyrighted works: "Mockingbird," by Inez Foxx and Charlie Foxx, additional lyrics by James Taylor. © 1963, 1974 (copyrights renewed) EMI Unart Catalog Inc. All rights reserved. Used by permission of Warner Bros. Publications U.S. Inc., Miami, Florida; "Windy," words and music by Ruthann Friedman. Copyright © 1967 Irving Music, Inc. Copyright renewed. All rights reserved. Used by permission.

PUBLISHER'S NOTE: This is a work of fiction. Names, characters, places, and incidents either are the product of the author's imagination or are used fictitiously, and any resemblance to actual persons, living or dead, business establishments, events, or locales is entirely coincidental.

LIBRARY OF CONGRESS CATALOGING-IN-PUBLICATION DATA
Sims, Stacy.
    Swimming naked : a novel / Stacy Sims.
        p.   cm.
    ISBN 0-670-03290-5 (alk. paper)
        I. Title.
PS3619.I5665S95 2004
813'.6—dc21   2003052593

This book is printed on acid-free paper. ∞

Printed in the United States of America
Designed by Carla Bolte

To my loving parents

Swimming Naked

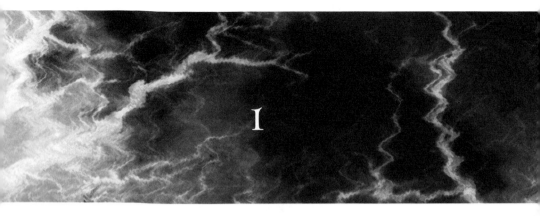

I

Every summer, my family rented the same small house on the same mosquito-covered lake in the same small town in Canada, several hours north of Toronto. The idea was to drive all the way in one day, packing the station wagon the night before so that we could leave at 4:00 a.m.

My older sister, Anna, and I would crawl into the back of the wagon, still half asleep, wearing our pajamas and our untied gym shoes, which had been put on our feet before we began our zombielike walk to the car. Anna walked a few steps ahead of me, both of us carrying our pillows. The only sound of the start of the journey was the crunch of the gravel in the driveway under our feet as we shuffled to the car. We lay down on top of our sleeping bags, which had been unzipped and spread out one on top of the other; hers Tony-the-tiger striped and mine a jumble of blue and yellow daisies. My parents were completely silent as they loaded a final bag of towels, a cooler, my mother's purse. They were often silent. It just seemed more noticeable against the quiet of the night.

They were exciting in their own way, the moments that marked the beginning of the trip: the smell of the coffee rising from a thermos in the front seat, the sound of the lighter popping out of its hole, glowing hot to light the first of my parents' many cigarettes. We fell back asleep almost immediately and woke up a couple of hours later in a different state. Anna and I opened our eyes at the exact same time, blinking hard and taking each other in for a second before looking around to remember where we were: trapped in our parents' silent, smelly car. We were desperate to go to the bathroom and sat up, suddenly wide-awake, clamoring for my father to stop the car. I don't remember my mother ever driving on vacation.

My father finally stopped, passing, as always, at least one viable exit before giving in. We ran clumsily to the bathroom, trying to avoid stepping on our untied shoelaces. When we finally got there, I went into my own stall, dutifully pushing the rusty bolt into the rusty lock. Anna shouted, "Don't sit down!" I said, "Okay," then sat down on the toilet, anticipating the moment when the pee came rushing out, warming my insides and sending a shiver through my body. I wiped and then got another piece of toilet paper to wipe my legs and bottom where they had rested against the porcelain. Anna made me wash my hands. I wiped mine dry on my pajamas and waited an eternity for Anna as she dried her hands under

the loud air dryer. Finally, we ran back to the car, our legs flailing out crazylike, exaggerated and goofy, around the flying shoelaces. We climbed into the back again and sat Indian-style, facing front, Anna behind the back of my father's head and me behind my mother. The backseat created a barrier between them and us and was filled with our luggage, since Anna and I took over the serious storage space for our travel bedroom.

Last year my father had attempted to tie the luggage to the top of the station wagon. It was an unpleasant memory for all of us, Anna in particular. We had been driving along for hours, well into the trip to the lake. The cigarette smoke had commingled for hours with the smell of Dentyne gum and my farts. "I can't help it!" I would maintain, each and every time. The windows were up because it was raining, keeping every stinky odor trapped inside the car. Anna was teaching me a trick with string, something far more complicated than Cat's Cradle and likely made up and not a real trick at all.

We heard a scraping noise then a thump on the top of the car. We looked back to see several pieces of luggage flying and a colorful jumble of clothes swirling in the rain. This was seconds before the luggage and the clothes hit the grille of a huge truck behind us. By the time my father pulled the car to the side of the road, the truck was long gone and with it went most of Anna's favorite summer clothes. She had insisted on packing her things in her own Sleeping Beauty luggage. Two other pieces of luggage had flown off with Anna's, but my father had rescued them from the highway—beaten but intact and still locked shut. The only thing he had been able to save from the now-missing Sleeping Beauty suitcase was her hot-pink bathing suit.

We watched out of the back of the station wagon as my father stood by the side of the road in the pouring rain, waiting until there was a break in traffic. He darted out one last time and grabbed Anna's muddy, wet bathing suit. When he got back in the car he handed it to her, torn strap and all. She cried the rest of the way to the lake, clutching the mangled, flimsy fabric in her hand. She wore that bathing suit, with the strap reattached with a safety pin, for the rest of the vacation but never entirely recovered. Her eyes were filled with misery for a whole week.

After that, the suitcases always stayed in the middle seat, along with the food. The suitcases were stacked on the seat; the food was in a cooler on the floor. My mother kept a special bag in the front seat filled with car toys and snacks. The butterscotch Lifesavers, candy cigarettes, and gum would be gone within the first hour or two of the trip. The comic books, crossword puzzles, and secret writing tablets would each seem hugely exciting for about ten minutes. We had to beg for everything.

It was a part of the deal, an attempt to make us feel as though we were a happy little family, with rituals and everything. After having just eaten doughnuts and orange juice, we began to whine for a car toy and a treat. My mother looked to my father, as though she actually wanted his participation in the decision. She said, "Frank, what do you think?" smiling in this sappy, unfamiliar way, then sighing and shaking her head, as though giving in to something seriously against her better judgment. I don't think my father even realized he had been part of the act. He just drove and smoked cigarettes, occasionally looking into the rearview mirror, saying to us in the mirror's reflection, always a little too loud but not quite a shout, "We'll be there in about a week and a half. You girls good with that?"

I knew somehow that these moments were important to my mother. And I worked really hard to play along with the vacation game. Anna totally bought the program. She was lying down on her stomach on her side of the station wagon, with her head toward the tailgate, reading Archie comic books with a concentration that was nearly impenetrable. I swung my body around, so I could lie next to her. I wrote on the secret message pad, scribbling all the worst words I could think of. I wrote "bad" then ripped the gray plastic up so the newly visible black letters disappeared. I did it so Anna couldn't see what I had written and because it had a built-in, nasty sound.

I wrote another word, "dam," then ripped up the plastic, *schwip.* This didn't get a response, so I scrawled only a line on the pad, just to have something to erase.

"Stop it, Lucy," Anna said, her head still cocked, perkily, from her own secret attempts to mimic Veronica or Betty. She could read to herself but she always moved her lips and was silently dramatic in doing so, tossing her head or smiling shyly, whatever the character demanded of her.

Schwip went the message pad. "I'm just doing secret messages," I added quickly, loud enough so my mother could hear.

Schwip, schwip, schwip, I demonstrated, pulling the plastic up repeatedly. "See, it makes this sound," demonstrating *schwip* again, "when you erase the words," adding, "Mom, that's how it works," because I knew we were only seconds away from her intervention.

"Mom, she is doing it on purpose," Anna complained. "I can't concentrate," she added, sighing as though she were reading something terribly important.

Schwip. I had written "fat head" and needed to erase it.

"Lucy, stop." My mother caved in so easily. I knew it had to do with the noise. I could sit and smash bugs, heartlessly squishing ant after ant after ant. Or write in marker all over my body. Or trace my name with the edge of a wet, slimy, half-eaten Lifesaver on the back of the station wagon window. As long as I didn't make any noise, I could get away with murder.

I tried writing only at the very edge of the secret message pad, so erasing would only make a tiny noise, *schw, schw.*

"You aren't writing anything at all," Anna reprimanded, her voice raised. "Mom!"

"Stop it, Lucy. Give that to me right now." My mother unbuckled her seat belt and turned full around, her left arm reaching all the way back into our space now, hand open, palm up to confiscate the secret message pad.

I gave it to her, swinging it down against her palm, *swack.* I am sure it didn't hurt. It was the noise that did me in.

"Get up here right now," my mother warned, as I retreated to the farthest corner of the station wagon, knees against my chest and arms wrapped tightly around my knees. I looked out the side window, suddenly fascinated with the passing scenery. "Now," my mother repeated. Her voice had lost all of its vacation charm.

Anna did as she always did. She acted as though she had no part whatsoever in the drama unfolding in front of her; the drama she created by telling on me. She kept reading her comic book, twirling her hair around her right finger, crossing and uncrossing her legs at the ankles. She never once looked at me. She kept reading; mouthing the words, raising her eyebrows, and wriggling her shoulders for Veronica's southern accent.

I knew it wasn't the biggest kind of trouble. All I had to do was to go forward and sit, squished, in the middle seat for a while. But I wasn't going to give in to my mother so easily. She had her games, I had mine.

"If you smoke, you'll die," I said quietly, almost a whisper. It made Anna look up and over at me, startled and concerned.

"What did you say?" my mother asked. "Get up here right now or we're pulling over."

"You are going to die," I said. "You smoke."

Anna was undone. She covered her ears with her hands and started crying, saying, "Mom, please, make her stop it."

My mother slammed her hand down on the top of the seat, making my father jump. "Pull over, Frank. Now." I heard the car move from pavement to crunchy gravel so I crawled quickly toward the middle seat, climbing over and wedging myself between the suitcases and the door on the passenger side of the car. I looked sullenly out the window and whimpered just the tiniest little bit. "Well, you are," I whispered.

The car moved back from the gravel to the pavement and we drove along, silently. After a few minutes, I felt my mother's hand on my knee. She had squeezed her arm between her seat and the door, curving it behind her to tap my leg. I ignored her, looking out the window for at least three taps of her vacation-manicured finger against my leg. Then I felt something tickle my leg. I looked down and saw that my mother had a stick of gum, still wrapped, and was running it up and down against my leg—a peace offering. In that moment, I knew I had won a round, but I was too much in love with her to care.

2

"You look so pretty," my mother claimed, for the very first time in our thirty-year relationship.

I had just come from the bathroom, which, like every hospital bathroom I had had the pleasure to pee in, was lit up like the inside of a spaceship. That's why I knew for certain that I looked like a heroin addict, with huge dark circles under my eyes, my filthy hair peeking out from under my baseball cap. The bathroom light cast a greenish, eerie glow that illuminated the metal handrails, the sanitary napkins, and the large-scale diapers. It had more open floor space than anywhere in the rest of my mother's cramped hospital room. It had to accommodate a wretched scenario, where my mother, say, would need a nurse, or worse, me, to assist her as she went to the bathroom. And I would have to drag along all of her attendant, ubiquitous machines with their thin yellow tubes, arranging them alongside of her as though I were merely straightening out the fabric of a long, taffeta gown, pins in my teeth and murmuring, "There, there, now that's better."

She said it again. "You look pretty, honey. Where is your hair? You used to have such nice hair." And with that, she closed her eyes, completely stoned on hospital drugs.

She had been in and out of consciousness all day. She was only fifty-eight, but she looked absolutely ancient, like Miss Jane Pittman at the end, only white. She was technically lying in her bed but was practically sitting up. The head of her bed had been jacked up high for some unknown medical reason. I was unwilling to mess with the setup of anything. I didn't want to be responsible for making my mother look or feel any worse than she already did. So I continued with the task at hand.

"It says here 'death in the twentieth-century society is treated much like sex was treated in the nineteenth century. The subject is avoided, especially with children. The opposite is also true: in the nineteenth century, death was discussed as freely and openly as sex is today.' " I read cheerfully, picking back up where I had been reading to her from one of the thirteen or so books I had found in the small, exceedingly well lit and reasonably well stocked Boca Siesta library.

"What do you think of that, Mom?" I asked my sexless, death-heavy mother.

One of the nurses came into the room. She gave me a sympathetic smile as I closed my book. Her name was Eileen and she was tolerable. The rest of the staff here hates me a tiny bit less now. I entered their world under extreme duress. It was not my idea to leave my job and move to Florida to watch my mother die. And it certainly was not my idea that it would be me and not Anna sitting here day after day, desperately trying to impart some sort of a death philosophy to my godless mother while tending to her hair, her nails, her sores, her pans, her tubes, her shriveling, wasted, stinky body. She was the incredible shrinking woman with me by her side. Anna was missing in action.

"How is she today?" Eileen asked, posing the requisite question.

I answered, "Terrific. Not a moan or a groan. The morphine is doing its groove thing." Not the requisite answer. But Eileen just shook her head, smiling, and went about her business of tapping tubes and measuring body fluids.

The doctors had ascertained and duly reported thirteen days ago, exactly five days after I had arrived in Florida, that my mother's lack of attention to her cancer had led to an incurable, inoperable, untreatable prognosis. "At this point we can do our best to manage her pain," they told me. "You might want to look into hospice," they said. They didn't mention that getting a bed in a hospice required serious money and/or serious connections. There were a lot of people dying in Florida.

I quickly came to believe that I represented pure evil to them. The story must have been in secret doctor code on all the charts. They had penned in Rx language in their indecipherable handwriting that I was the daughter that left her mother to die, that I had not been aware she had lost thirty pounds from her thin frame and had been coughing up important organic matter daily for two months.

One of the doctors must have read a bit further in the chart, all the way to the part where I claim she never told anyone, and thought it sounded plausible enough for further examination.

"Mrs. Greene, why didn't you tell anyone you were sick?" he asked.

"I wasn't that sick," my mother asserted, through clenched teeth, trying to focus on her answer rather than her considerable pain.

I silently gestured "See?" to the doctor. He shook his head and clicked his pen to punctuate the end of the conversation. He had a thick southern accent and a golfer's tan. We were the pasty white, inactive northerners. My mother was one of the unfortunate snowbirds who had not seen her reflection in the window of a sad, little white-stucco Florida condominium and had flown right into the glass, falling, wings broken, to the hot pavement below.

I had gotten the call from my mother's thick-tongued, foreign-born neighbor a couple of weeks ago. Bella was, in her words, "gravely concerned about Fay." And further irritated that "you people have just left her here to die." I honestly didn't think that is what "we people" had in mind when we wrote the check every month to the mortgage company for the Florida condominium, enticingly situated near the golf course and a few minutes' walk from the pool and restaurant. It was a sad, low-rent gated community, but Fay seemed happy enough. At least that is what she implied during the five or so minutes we spoke once a month.

It had taken several long and confusing phone calls with Bella for me to ascertain my mother was seriously ill. When I couldn't get either of them, Bella or my mother, to give me a doctor's name or phone number, I booked a flight. When I first saw her I couldn't believe that Bella, or anyone for that matter, hadn't phoned sooner. She was skeletal. But after I was there a few days and had met the rest of her friends in the complex, I could imagine how it would have been hard for them to tell that her demise was more imminent and forceful than their own, particularly since my mother was far younger than most of them and had neglected to mention her cancer. She pretended, instead, to have been overzealous with her low-fat diet. They all looked notably feeble, for a variety of reasons, and their ailments were bandied about like some lighthearted game of toss. Bella, the one who called, went three times a week for dialysis. "All this fancy new insulin," she would say, "it isn't going to help me one bit. I'm lucky just to be able to see."

My mother is dying, and she is dying with a vengeance, not in the naive sense of "we're all dying." If you hear someone say that, you can be pretty sure they have never seen someone in the active process of dying from cancer, particularly a lung cancer that has metastasized practically everywhere. Stage Four. Her body is in a constant state of pain; it shrinks and recoils but remains in the path of a relentless cancer that has run amok. It was a forest fire during high wind season. And yes.

Swimming

Naked

It was a cigarette that started the fire. The fact that I am not only a negligent daughter but also a smoking one has not gone unnoticed here at the hospital. The nasty habit adds a hefty bonus onto my already high score on the bad daughter chart. On occasion I happily spy one of her nurses, the overweight, fat-ankled one, huddled in the back corner of the garden, smoking quickly before dousing herself with perfume and popping mints on her way back inside. I smile warmly at her. She never looks at me.

I have also come to understand that a hospital is not a great place to attempt to die, peacefully or otherwise. Here, by decree, they are in the business of keeping people alive, which is a terrific thing unless one is truly ready to die. Even having gotten my mother to sign all the living will papers and the do-not-resuscitate orders, I still felt a bit terrified that if she had a stroke or something I would be doing duty for the rest of my life, tending to her in some vegetative state. I imagined that after the hospital would have saved what was left of her life, the cancer would slow, and the Lucy and Fay show would play out in some bleak, dark room for bloody ever.

That is why I was constantly on alert for some critical medical news that might be delivered when I wasn't paying attention. Suddenly, as I would be nodding off in a terribly uncomfortable chair next to my mother's bed, a troupe of doctors would begin an astonishingly fast and unintelligible discussion of my mother's case. My mother was absolutely invisible to them; she had Stage Four cancer. I was visible only when I insisted upon it. When I asked a question, they would look at me as though I had interrupted the final act of a serious play. I stood up from my chair in the front row of their theater, a heckler. And even though I was there around the clock, either bedside or outside in the small garden smoking, I simply didn't read as a formidable caregiver, someone they should take seriously. I looked like a Yankee troublemaker, like a girl who might hang out with bikers or intellectuals, either swigging beer or sipping espresso. They imagined tattoos and leather and girl-on-girl sex, not tan lines and white cotton and girl-on-tennis-pro sex.

This could be because I wore nothing but black. My Florida, casual, hospital-going outfit consisted of black Keds, black leggings, a black T-shirt, a black ball cap with what appeared to be an anarchy symbol on it. It was actually a symbol made up by an artist as a title to an exhibit I had organized. The artist would contend it had nothing to do with anarchy. But the artist was also only twenty-two years old and didn't know any better. I thought the work was just good enough and the artist just hot enough for me to ignore his lack of self-awareness and intellect. The critics disagreed. But we're talking Cleveland, not New York, so his career and mine flourished anyway, flourished being a relative concept. I got a hat and a few months of enthusiastic sex during my studio visits before moving on to other artists and a series of critically acclaimed (acclaim also being a relative concept) exhibits entitled *Shutter.* He got a catalogue and a series of new girlfriends, two of whom, fully pierced and very young, had installed his work under my direction. Everyone walked away happy, feeling exhilarated from an experience that felt more important than it actually was. The art did this. Fucking on the floor in a dark-room, with an artist's newly printed photos hanging above your head, felt like an intellectual rite of passage rather than what it was, which was fucking on the floor in a darkroom.

So while I was a noted curator of photography in the Mid-west, that distinction held little use for most real-world appli-cations. I had, however, taken to the job of finding a death philosophy for my mother like a duck to water. It made me uneasy that my mother was going to die and had neither a firm belief nor a tentative sense of hope about how the whole thing worked, intellectually or spiritually. I just wanted her to consider something, anything. I had the idea she should have a notion, a wish, a fantasy about where she was going when she died. While I didn't start out with a strong preference for one belief over another, finding certain Eastern notions as reason-able or ridiculous as Western ones, I did make a few curatorial decisions and, in fact, was moving the whole thesis more toward, say, Tibet. I edited out the frightening edicts straight away, like the "Roman Ritual for Catholic Christians." The summary I read advertised a long and complicated process as a "forearming against the terrors of that last passage." It seemed an awful lot of work for what would likely be, at best, a long shot at the sweet hereafter. I figured my mother had a far bet-ter chance of attaining a decent enough state of mind at the time of her death to ratchet up her karma for rebirth into an equal or higher realm. I hoped the worst-case scenario might find her back in the animal realm; a lazy cat perhaps, putting her disdainful, dismissive posture to good use for at least one more lifetime.

The hospital administrators didn't know what to think of me and my formidable stack of death books. They asked once about other family members who might be able to help with her care. They posed this question to me when I was out of my mother's room, hunting for apple juice in the small refrigerator by the nurses' stand. I told them there was no one else. This was, in a sense, true.

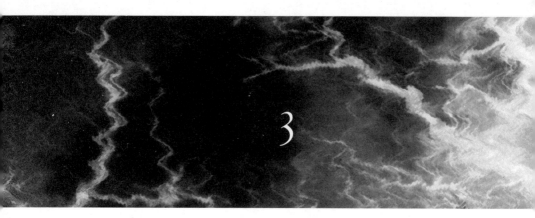

3

It was almost dark by the time we made it to the house on the lake, having barely survived the car ride. The air-conditioning hardly cooled the front half of the car, so by the end of the trip, Anna and I were so hot and uncomfortable we were limp. Our newly purchased vacation T-shirts and shorts, which we had wriggled into while lying on our sleeping bags, were wet with sweat and stuck to our bodies. Our hair was matted into strange asymmetrical styles. Anna's springy curls had been flattened out on one side and puffed up on the other. My hair hung in two wilting ponytails. The heat, our steady diet of candy, and the incarcerated cigarette smoke rendered us nearly mute. I mustered a groan as I attempted to peel my soggy clothes away from my skin. I felt like I was trapped in a terrarium on wheels.

Anna asked, weakly, "How much farther? How many more miles?"

"We're almost there," assured my mother, which was not comforting at all because she had said this the last seventeen times or so when either Anna or I had asked.

"How many more miles?" I asked, weaker even than Anna. I often wished to be more pitiful-sounding than her. "For real?" I begged.

"Only ten miles," my father reported. "As long as it takes for me to get to work," he clarified with information that was totally useless to Anna and me since we had never been to where he works.

"Mom!" we implored, weakly, together. She knew what we wanted and gave it to us, finally, the real answer put in such a way so that we could understand what she was saying. "As long as it takes to get to the place that cuts your hair."

My mother had a way of withholding herself from us that was in direct proportion to how much we needed her. It always felt like we were asking far too much from her, even when we just wanted her to wake up from her nap to look at a picture or to help with scissors. Sometimes she would get mad at us and yell something that made no sense even to her, I'll bet. Most often, she would just hold herself back from us, her whole self or her words, and make us wait. This required a sort of patience that Anna had a lot more of than I did. She could wait forever.

We finally approached the area along a desolate stretch of highway where we engaged in another summer ritual, "The Finding of the Hidden Driveway." I would see signs all the time that said "Watch for Hidden Drive," and then would see the driveway easily and wonder why it was said to be hidden. The driveway to this house was truly hidden. The only thing we knew for sure was that we had to be on the side of the car behind my dad to find it, and that if we made it to the bridge, we had missed it. It was just dark enough for it to be almost impossible to find the entrance. I was the first to spot it and yelled, "There it is!" I was so happy to be there, finally, and even happier to have found it first.

"No, I don't think so, honey," my mother murmured, squinting her eyes and holding her hands over them, like she was looking for ships far in the distance. But I was right. My father was the first to realize we had just passed it and slammed on the brakes to back up. I fell into Anna, who fell into the back of the seat as our heads collided. So we arrived at the lake house with the typical fanfare. We emerged from the back of the station wagon soaked with sweat and crying, my mother swiping at our clothes, making little noises of disgust as she brushed off the crumbs of a day's worth of junk food. My father leaned up against the side of the car, lighting another cigarette. He looked at the house admiringly and announced, "Well, we made it." He made it sound as arduous a journey as it had been.

The house, illuminated by a single light on the back porch, had a ramshackle quality to it that made it feel welcoming. I knew what it would smell like when the door opened. Our house smelled like bacon and cigarette smoke. This house smelled more like my aunt Martha's apartment. Her apartment had a peculiar musty odor and was so covered in cat hair I was certain I couldn't get in trouble for messing up one single thing there. It was already a mess to begin with.

Aunt Martha always called me "honey" and never asked me to take off my shoes. She never even seemed to notice when my face was covered in chocolate or dirt or something else sticky. I stayed with her when my mother and Anna went to run important errands. When my mother came to get me she would look at me in horror and start cleaning me up by licking her fingers and wiping my face with her bare, saliva-covered hands. She couldn't even wait to get to the sink for some running water and a napkin. Anna would stand at the door, looking around the apartment with her eyes as big as doughnuts, her mouth wide open.

I didn't think it was so bad. It was just messy and Aunt Martha didn't seem to think it important to throw things away. That's why the newspapers were stacked as high as I was tall, creating narrow pathways throughout her apartment. "You never know when you might want to read something again," she would tell me. She also didn't seem to be in too much of a hurry to get rid of the remnants of her meals. There would be plates and plates stacked everywhere, defying gravity. One stack was so high it leaned like a sprung jack-in-the-box. I would hold my breath as I passed it. There were empty, dirty glasses too. They were everywhere, one to two on every surface, including the wobbly top of the highest stack of dirty plates. One day I saw her reach for a box on a high shelf. She pulled down a brand-new set of glasses, six more to leave around to disgust my mother and Anna.

Swimming

Naked

My mother would always have something to give Aunt Martha, usually a letter for her that had been delivered to our house. She was my father's sister and had a mysterious life my parents only spoke of in whispers. My mother would clear her throat if I walked in while they were talking about her. Once I heard "disgusting" and "in the newspaper, for God's sake." I assumed they were talking about something gross they found rotting amid one of the stacks of papers in her apartment.

This house, with its slightly unpleasant smell and no cat hair, was intended for summer people doing messy summer things. You could come in with your feet wet and covered with little pieces of cut grass, since there wasn't any carpeting to worry about. My mother swept the wooden floors constantly, but it wasn't a hurried, angry sweep. She didn't even yell at us. It seemed she carried the broom with her at all times, ready to start swinging it, *swoosh,* against the painted and chipped yellow wood floors in the kitchen. She just went on talking about the summer corn or the new neighbors and swept away all the sure signs of our vacation. She would stop her sweeping and take a little break. She would stand with the broom in front of her, leaning into it with her hands clasped around the handle in household prayer. She would look out the window toward the lake and say, "I could stay here all year." Then she would shake her head, as though to rouse herself from this silly dream, and resume sweeping.

My father fumbled with the keys to the house as Anna and I jumped up and down, holding ourselves between our legs. Seemingly half of my childhood was spent waiting to go to the bathroom. Hearing the water, lapping up against the rocks down at the end of the lawn, didn't help at all. He finally got the door open and we slammed through it. I made it to the downstairs bathroom first and shut the door behind me. Anna punched it once before running upstairs to the other bathroom.

The summerhouse had so many interesting things to look at. In this bathroom alone, there was a striped rug made from old rags on the floor over a pink-painted wood floor. The toilet lid had a pink shag rug cover and there was a matching pink shag igloo for the extra toilet paper that sat on top of the tank behind me. I could reach the drawer to the right of the sink. I opened it to examine its contents for the first of many such inspections. It contained all sorts of things you wouldn't think would go in the same place. There was some multicolored yarn. I pulled on it and it kept coming and coming from the back of the drawer. I wadded it up and put it back in. There were three matchbooks. I didn't touch those. That would be asking for it. There was a card, a three of hearts, and a ball from jacks, but no jacks. There was a cardboard tube from a roll of toilet paper and a tiny bottle of shampoo. I stuck my hand in the drawer to stir around the contents to see what else I might find. Just then, I heard my mother outside the door. She tapped on it. I could imagine her out there, her ear to the door, tapping with the back of her knuckle. I got up and flushed the toilet just as I shut the drawer to hide the sound of all that mixed up stuff sliding around. I didn't know exactly why I would be in trouble for looking in the drawer, but I probably would be, so I covered my tracks just in case.

I opened the door and could tell immediately the house was working its own pink-painted-wood magic on my mother. She had that summer look. She would describe the house to her friends with words I loved to hear: "louvered, cantilevered, beveled." I knew our house, our rest-of-the-year house, didn't have any of those things or else my mother wouldn't speak those words with such reverence, making the concepts themselves mysterious and wonderful. As I was trying to slide by her past the bathroom door, she leaned down to me and whispered, "Meet me at the last rock."

I stood there stunned. What was she saying? She repeated herself. "Meet me at the last rock," and added, "I'll tell Dad and Anna to unpack the car." I was thrilled and confused by my mother's invitation. She turned me around and gently pushed me toward the back porch. "Go. I'll be there in a minute."

I could hear her speaking to my father and Anna but couldn't make out her words as I walked down the path toward the rock beach. I was as scared of the dark as the super-scared Anna but I would never admit it to anyone. I shut my eyes and took a few steps, preferring the dark of my own making to the dark of the night. I would open them, make sure I was on the path, and then shut them tight and take a few more steps. It was a short walk to the rock beach by day, but a long one by night, eyes closed, a few steps at a time. My mother caught up with me before I even reached the rocks.

STACY

SIMS

She took my hand and said, "Enjoying the stroll?" I looked to see if she was teasing me then looked back to see if Anna was coming too. "Don't worry, honey. It's just us." She smiled at me and squeezed my hand. It seemed she was saying something to me where the words were the same as what she actually meant. I was speechless with suspicion. Where was she taking me? Why was she acting so nice? How come she asked me and not Anna?

She gently pulled me in front of her and put both hands on my shoulders, guiding me onto the rocks. We climbed over several large rocks, almost boulders, to get to the pebbly part of the beach, where the big rocks had been worn into tiny smooth stones. We took off our shoes and headed toward the lighthouse. The last rock marked where the beach became impassable and you had to cut up into the woods for a time before coming out again, near the public beach.

When we got there, my mother turned to me and said, "I have a surprise. A secret for you and me." I had no idea what this could be. My mind, first a blank, suddenly reeled with ideas. A pony, a red pencil-holder, lipstick, a tire swing, my own room, candy necklaces, a kitten, TV in the morning. My mother began to take off her shirt, a peculiar smile on her face. I was beginning to be afraid. She said, "Come on. We're going skinny-dipping." I stood there frozen. I didn't know what she meant. She said, "We are going to go swimming without any clothes on."

I started to take off my shorts. They were still sticking to me, wet from the sweat of the trip and now even more damp because I was sweating again, this time more than a little afraid of my mother. I didn't ever trust her much, but I knew what I was up against, most of the time. She was usually so predictable. This was completely out of the ordinary for the mother I had come to know. Suddenly I was with this odd, nice woman, this reckless person who sought me out for a special, secret adventure for just the two of us. She wanted to go skinny-dipping. My mother wanted to go swimming naked in the lake, with me.

I looked back down the beach toward the house. I could barely make out the lights. I was standing there with my shorts around my knees as my mother finished undressing, tossing her underwear on top of the pile of her clothes with a great, dramatic sweep of her hand. I couldn't remember ever seeing my mother naked. She presented herself to me, in the moonlight. She ran her hands down the sides of her body then took a deep breath and raised her eyebrows, as though to indicate "Okay, here goes." She reached up and took the pins out of her hair and dropped them on the beach. She threw the last two into the water. She shook her hair and it fell around her shoulders, black and wild against her skin.

She briefly became the mother I knew as she pulled my shirt over my head, strangling me as usual and indifferent to my cries of agony. She helped me pull my shorts all the way off. I held on to her bare shoulder as I stepped on one leg of the shorts, then the other, to be totally free of them. I tried not to look at her but I couldn't stop myself. She was so beautiful, this new mother. She took the rubber bands out of my hair, one on each side, both times pulling out a hair or two. I didn't say a word, even when it hurt, but instead shook my hair loose and free like she had done.

She grabbed my hand and we began to run toward the water. It was shockingly cold, but the shock was no greater than anything that had preceded it. It was just one more stinging sensation that, while completely foreign, had a hint of something familiar to it. We ducked under the water and came back up to swim side by side. I paddled a half stroke, half dog paddle. My mother moved her arms in circles around her, elegantly pushing the water forward and backward, toward her, then away from her. The water felt slippery against my skin. It felt very different from bathwater. We were silent for a long time. My mother flipped over on her back, and floated on top of the water, as still as could be. I paddled and tried not to swallow any water so I could look at her. She was shimmering in the moonlight. My legs got so tired I started to go under. I started coughing from the water, and my mother came over in one smooth mermaid move and pulled me to her. She swam, holding me, until she could reach the bottom. She stood up and held me like I was only a baby. I had my arms around her back, limp against her warm wet skin; my feet reached her knees practically. She walked through the water slowly, rubbing my wet hair against my back and kissing me on the head, every few steps or so.

She put me down on a big flat rock and told me we had to dry off before we put our clothes back on. She climbed up next to me and we lay there, looking up at the stars. She began

Swimming

Naked

to tell me what stars she could identify, naming constellations left and right, another mysterious, hidden skill. I peeked over at her and watched her lips moving in the moonlight, chanting, "Hydrus, Lacerta, Orion, Andromeda." I didn't say a word. I looked back up at the sky and wondered who else knew there was a secret person inside my mother.

4

I WAS LYING beside the pool at my mother's condominium, covered up with a patchwork of small, white pool towels. They were tiny, the towels, more of a size to dry hair than to spread out on a lounge chair or wrap around a dripping wet body. I wasn't interested in sunning myself or swimming, truth be told. I was so sick of the fluorescent-lit world of the hospital, I craved some natural light. I simply had to endure the salty Florida breezes, swaying palms, and tiny towels to get it. The heat was another story entirely, its own dark force of nature. It was unthinkable to me that people would live with this heat by choice. I had on a T-shirt and jeans and my black baseball cap and had put the towels over my feet, arms, hands, and neck to keep my very white self from obtaining a brutal sunburn. The towels beneath me kept slipping off the white and green slats of the lounge chair, leaving a sweaty striped pattern on my back where the rubberized bands stuck to me. I had

29

two weighty, academic books beside me and was deeply engrossed in a third—a dog-eared and mildly titillating romance novel I found in the pool cabana.

I was, theoretically, finishing my master's thesis while on duty with my mother. They were calling this time in hell my sabbatical. My therapist, Dr. Bergman, had been nearly gleeful when I had revealed the details of my topic to her. It was called *Transformative Acts: The Shock of the Moment.* I was comparing performance art to photography and maintained that certain photographers, Mapplethorpe, Goldin, Sherman, for example, and Arbus were merely documenting performance in a single, lasting frame. I had been an Arbus freak for as long as I could remember; this little detail having been recently pried out of me by my therapist.

My mother had taken us to the museum when I was six and Anna was eight. Every once in a while my mother would attempt some out-of-the-ordinary experience, which was usually so out of her ordinary experience she wouldn't know exactly what to do once we were there. I think she would like to have been the kind of mother who took us to museums, stopped at historical markers on the highway, or went on long nature walks. So she did. It's just that once at the museum, at the historic marker, or on the nature walk, she didn't know quite what to do except to finish it all very quickly. She would say, "Hmm. Would you look at that. Okay, ready girls?"

Mainly, it seemed, she was on the lookout for a good place to smoke. She would call out to us, "Now, *here* is a nice bench" as though it were something of great importance, artistically, historically, or naturally. We would run to see and find her clicking closed her brown leather cigarette case, a single Pall Mall in hand. She would pat the bench beside her, looking pleased with herself. Anna would run to sit to her left, leaving me her right side, her smoking side, which meant I had to keep some distance unless I wanted to swallow her smoke.

The day my mother took us to the museum turned out to be no different. My sister had fallen for *Cupid and Psyche.* In her world, this painting had everything going for it: a palace, an ornate bed, winged love, and the pièce de résistance, a big butterfly hovering over a naked couple, a randy-looking boy cherub and his smitten gal pal. While my mother stood with a group of touring women miming her relationship to Anna and me, I snuck off to the modern gallery.

I remember being struck by the fact that the only person in the room was a man writing something in a small brown book. It had seemed odd to me. So I decided to sit on a bench for a while to investigate this: a man in a museum with a notebook.

There was a stack of papers and books on the bench beside me. They belonged to the mystery man, who must have been a curator of some sort. I recall the moment I saw the cover of the book, unveiled to me slowly as I moved some papers out of the way. It was a photo of a girl wearing a white headband, just like the one I was wearing that day. I had pushed the paper a little farther and seen another girl in a white headband, who looked just like, nearly exactly like, the other girl in the white headband. I had never seen actual evidence of twins before and had found it mesmerizing. They were dressed alike and they looked alike. But somehow they were completely different. It had been an exciting discovery.

I picked up the book, the seminal book of Arbus's work, and opened it. I remember seeing some old naked people. It was as gross a picture then as it is now, and I had known somehow it would get me in trouble if my mother saw it, the women's big, saggy boobs and his fat, hairy stomach. I had turned the page. It had been the photo of the girl standing in the fog holding a basket, in a fancy dress and a flower headband and a coat made out of white feathers that really grabbed me. She had spooky eyes and wild hair like Anna. I had been so engrossed in my examination of the photograph I didn't hear the curator approach the bench.

"I'm not sure you should be looking at that book," he had said nervously, pushing his glasses up his nose with one pointy, long finger. I had assured him I had already seen the naked people.

"I'm just not sure Arbus is everybody's cup of tea," he had said to me, which at the time made no sense at all as I didn't know what a bus and a cup of tea had to do with anything. To this day, I see a yellow school bus and a cup of piping hot tea in "See Jane Run"–style illustrations every time I speak of Arbus. It seems mnemonic sacrilege.

I recalled for my shrink that once we were outside, having left the museum in our typical hurried fashion, we picked up the pace and moved quickly toward the lagoon on the museum grounds.

My mother found a bench and sat down exhausted from her hour of culture. She cupped her hand against the wind, lighting her cigarette. My sister did a modern dance by the edge of the lagoon, amid the pesky, encroaching Canada geese, that would seem to indicate she was not unmoved by her encounter with a naked girl and boy with wings. I was thinking about the Arbus pictures. Anna stopped suddenly and stared at me. I had been struck by how much she looked just like the girl in the photograph, how there was something beautiful in her own startled stare. I knew then that even though she was standing right in front of me and I could reach out and touch her, she wasn't really there at all. It might last only a minute or two, but Anna was in her own private dream place. She stood there, eyes fixed on me, gripping her crocheted purse with both hands in front of her like she was holding tight to the reins while trying to tame a wild pony.

I glanced over at my mother to see if she noticed. She was looking away, toward the other end of the pond, focused intently on an unknown object in the distance. She looked very glamorous, even in what she called her "ratty car coat." She chewed at the corner of her shiny, red mouth, screwing up her face and crinkling her forehead above her black, movie star sunglasses. The geese started toward us, coming up behind Anna, in their silent, creepy way. It was a familiar family snapshot; Anna frozen, my mother detached, my father missing. I had stood and watched, waiting for one of the geese to snap at Anna's heels. Or for someone just to snap.

This little tale had brightened my therapist's day considerably. It was so "revealing" she believed and it gave us a handy little tool—the photograph as a device to recall critical moments in time. You can just imagine how excited she was by my own academic thesis as it was quite similar to her psychological thesis about me.

Plus, there was a lot of sex going on in the photographs I had chosen, some of it most often described as deviant. And let me tell you, there are a few words and phrases that will perk up any therapist, no matter how restrained and professional she might appear otherwise. It's a subtle, body language thing. One has to be as observant as, say, a psychologist to notice and process the detail. Any sex talk at all promotes a straightening of the spine. Any talk of behavior that might remotely fall into the category of sexual dysfunction yields an opening of the chest, the near touching of shoulder blades, and a deepening of the breath. It is a yogalike preparation for some serious shrink work. For my therapist, the idea that I had chosen to combine a sexual subplot with shocking, singular events equaled big, fat Wonder Bread crumbs in the forest of my psyche. I had been, in layman's terms, a hard nut to crack. The fact that I rarely discussed my sex life with her sent her psychologically scrambling for clues in Mapplethorpe's bullwhip and Goldin's addicts. These were red herrings, each and every one of them. I merely fucked men I didn't love. There was no one taking pictures of that; it was too commonplace. And it certainly wasn't something I cared to offer up to Dr. Bergman for her thesis about me.

I had been seeing Dr. Bergman for about a year and liked

her well enough. I gave in to this popular concept of "talking to someone" after years of successful avoidance. I didn't get there because of some clinically interesting event, at least not a recent one, but rather was worn down, drawn in, like some weary, reticent moth to Freud's eternal flame. I had been to see only one other therapist, a white-haired man my mother took my sister and me to see after my father's accident. For some reason, he saw the two of us together, as though our experiences and reactions would be exactly the same. Anna pretty much ran that show, stripping girl and boy dolls naked, smashing them up against each other while making "oh, ah, mmm, mmm" noises. He would have us play dress-up games with each other. I would have to put on a hat and a vest. Anna would then banish me from the kingdom. She would then tell the psychiatrist that I, Prince Eric, had perished in fire and she would never love again. I had tried on occasion to drum up an affectation or story that might interest him. Once I feigned terror of a yellow block in the shape of an isosceles triangle. When questioned, I could muster only choking noises so I held my breath instead. The psychiatrist looked at me as though completely irritated and said, "Oh, please stop that." I never was as psychologically interesting as my sister.

In fact my current therapist, Dr. Bergman, had to work really hard to keep focused on my issues and not my sister's. It was handy though to have someone to validate or nullify my own analytic abilities. My sister was a veritable treasure trove of neurotic detritus. It became sport to make a diagnosis of her.

And of course "we" talked about my mother, my dad, James, and Anna. "Our work" included lots of discovery from the old days, the years of my youth. With dark, deep pools of water and raging storms as metaphors for the varying degrees of my immersion into the ego, superego, or id of whatever we happened to be discussing, once a week, in a windowless room above a grocery store in Cleveland Heights, Dr. Bergman was intrigued by what my seaside sabbatical to nurse my mother, during hurricane season no less, might "bring up." She was downright enthusiastic the last session I had with her before leaving for Florida, using the snapshot device to help impart the importance of this upcoming imprint.

"It might be important to carry a photo of your moat dream. The water will be all around you and the castle may be beginning to show signs of wear," Dr. Bergman intoned, her hopeful posture belying her professional impassivity.

My solemn, ponderous look must have brightened her day considerably. I nodded slowly and wrote out a check to her, silent. I didn't have the heart to tell her she had assigned one of Anna's recurring dreams to my far less colorful psyche.

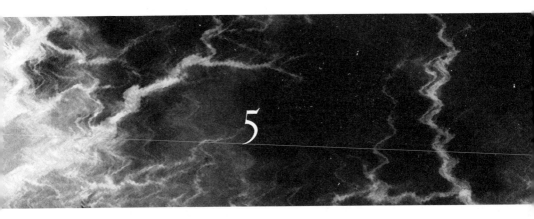

5

I WAS LYING on the floor of the porch. I had actually permitted Anna to dress me in one of her getups. I wore a green, silky slip that was about five times too big for me. It was the only thing that didn't make my skin hurt even more. My parents were leaving us home alone. "We were invited!" my mother offered, by way of explanation. Anna was tap-dancing for me, stomping loudly on the wooden porch floor in her cowboy boots, bathing suit, and floppy hat. When she quit clomping around, she started swinging her butt and slowly waving her arms in one of her Maria dance numbers. It was hard to tell if she was being Maria in the *Sound of Music* or Maria in *West Side Story*. Generally, her *Sound of Music* Maria was happier than her *West Side Story* Maria. But you could catch her in a silent rendition of "I Feel Pretty" and easily mistake one Maria for the other.

I stayed as still as I could, under the breeze of the creaky ceiling fan. My mother was certain it was going to fly right off one of these days. "Just you wait. You won't think it's funny when I'm decapitated," she warned as she and my father slammed the porch door behind them, leaving for the neighbors' house.

I didn't think anything was funny at that particular moment. Everyone had forgotten to put suntan lotion on me. That morning, we had hiked down to the beach. We packed up all of our things as though the beach was too far from the house to return for anything once we were there. I was lugging my towel, my flippers, and a small Styrofoam cooler full of ice when my mother gave me the very first sign of the whole vacation that acknowledged we had actually gone swimming naked together. As we passed the rock, she turned and looked over her tan shoulder and winked at me. Unfortunately, Anna saw the brief exchange and accidentally on purpose swung her cooler around, hitting me behind the knees so that I dropped to the ground. I told her to quit it, quietly, through clenched teeth. Even though my mother had just winked at me, she was a little unpredictable this morning. I had to watch out. You just never knew.

Anna had been angry ever since we disappeared that first night, leaving her to help my father unpack the car. She never asked me about it, though. She just watched my mother and me very carefully, every once in a while snapping her head around and narrowing her eyes at us, disapproving and suspicious. After I got back up, now behind everyone on the trek to the beach, Anna winked at me, imitating our mother, and then gave me the evil eye. Then she turned around and ran ahead to walk by our father, courting him for some unknown reason, singing sweet and clear, "Who's reaching out to capture a moment, everyone knows it's Windy."

By the time I caught up to everyone the blankets and towels were out, making one giant patchwork quilt of our stake to the rocky beach. My father appeared to have fallen instantly asleep in his folding beach chair, my mother was adjusting her huge beach hat, and Anna was trying, and failing, to skip stones. I dropped the cooler, flippers, and towel beside the blankets and ran down to try to skip my own rocks. I gave her one of my own deadly, silent glances. She stuck her tongue out at me then handed me a good skipping stone. Apparently, we were even.

We were both whipping rocks straight to the bottom of the lake, expecting each and every one to skim three or four or five times along the top of the water, when my mother started yelling at my father. She didn't actually shout. When she got mad her voice became higher and more shrill. I think that's why it sounded louder to us. She had a high-pitched whine that sent shivers up my spine and my hands to cover my ears. Maybe, like dogs with certain whistles, my sister and I were the only ones who could hear it. If my father did, he ignored it. She was standing over him with her hands on her hips. He kept his eyes closed. We looked up and down the beach to see if anyone else noticed my mother had gone nuts.

Swimming

Naked

"I asked you if you had packed the cigarettes and you said you did. Why did you say you did when you didn't?" she scolded.

"I am not going to walk all the way back to the house again. Every day I have to go back for something." She was getting madder by the second. "Excuse me!" she kicked him in the leg.

"Jesus Christ!" my father muttered, slamming his feet into his flip-flops. He headed back toward the house.

"Honey?" my mother called out, as nice as she could be. "Honey? Can you grab my blue sunglasses? I like those better."

She started toward us, a movie star's walk on a pebbly beach. She was wearing a shiny black bathing suit and high-heeled sandals. Her hair was pinned up into a French twist. Her lips looked slippery, slathered in bright red lipstick. The sunglasses she didn't like were jet-black. She would turn her head and nod, smiling, to her fans, the other families on the beach, as she passed them. Her face cracked once when she turned her foot on a large rock. She almost fell down. While she regained her footing, you could see the anger inside of her turning tricks on her face. Once she was up, everything was rearranged for something close to beauty. I looked at Anna. She was totally smitten.

"Christ, this place is turning into a dump," she complained through her beauty-pageant smile, picking up the sun-bleached wrapper from a Reese's Cup. She crumpled it up and held it tightly in her fist. "And that woman back there should not be wearing a bikini!" Then, without missing a beat, she asked, "What are you girls doing?" as sweet as she could be.

Given that my mother was suddenly noticing everything wrong with the beach and everyone on it that day, you would have thought she would have noticed I was getting redder and redder by the minute.

"Nothing," I said, while Anna, excited by her presence, gave it up without a fight.

"We're skipping stones! You need really flat ones and we can't find any more of them!" Anna revealed.

My mother bent over, running her long fingers lightly over the stones at the edge of the lake, combing for the perfect rock. Her bright red nail polish made her fingers look like beautiful fish, swimming, shimmering in the dark water. I thought she was going to do it again, show us some magical, hidden talent, like some sort of a witch; whether she was a good witch or a bad witch, I wasn't sure. I imagined she would pick up a perfect, flat stone, walk to the edge of the water, and set it sailing, skimming one, two, three, four, and a final, triumphant, five skips across the lake.

She stood upright after combing the stones for a while; drying her wet hands on her shiny black swimsuit, then examined her nails for any imperfection. "I never could skip stones," she confessed.

She walked back to the blankets and looked off toward the house to see if my father was returning yet. She shook her head slowly in her very disappointed way and turned back to look at us for a second. She was staring at us when she flopped down to a sitting position, her limbs and posture going totally limp. Anna and I looked at each other. My mother's posture looked familiar to us. It was our own, preadolescent signal of exasperation.

I prayed Anna would stay with me and play, but I knew she had to go to my mother. It was a part of their own silent pact. When my mother acted like a child, it was Anna's job to coax the mother back out of her. I watched Anna rubbing my mother's hair, murmuring something to her. Then I turned back around and began flinging stones straight back to the bottom of the lake, one dumb rock at a time.

6

"Lucy, i know you're there. Pick up," the message began. There was a long pause on my mother's answering machine before Anna spoke again.

"Fine. I'll talk to this stupid machine." Another long pause. I was already irritated. It was all right with me if she needed to pretend that I was merely vacationing in Florida, not answering the phone because I was too overcome from tanning and margaritas to move off the veranda. She could pretend to herself and her own team of specialists right through our mother's death and funeral as far as I was concerned. Even though it was a trademark of my family to ignore serious personal issues and, rather, to be constantly on alert for problems evident in other people, it made me crazy that she still expected me to engage in some inane conversation about a new recipe for party dip. I couldn't imagine that this was productive for either of us, for me to play along with her scenario that everything was right with the world while I alone watched our mother die. It was hard enough to keep up the charade with my mother that Anna was all right. That she and her husband were doing just great, really, and those girls, my God, what an adorable family.

I had been keeping up this pretense for weeks now, ever since the morning I put my mother in the hospital. The ambulance had just left her condominium and Bella had ambled toward me, crying. I fished around in my purse for my sunglasses and put them on in a hurry. Then I got busy putting my mother's suitcase and some magazines I had lifted from the condo's pool collection into my obnoxious rental car. I leaned way across the backseat as though I had quite a bit to arrange in there. I was not ready to deal with another old-world reprimand.

Bella had placed her swollen body between the door and the car, trapping me there. When I finally stood up, my back was pressed against her. The heat in the car merged with the heat of our bodies and the permanently heavy heat in the air. It felt like the slow-motion blast of a nuclear bomb. I felt sick. She moved back slightly, creating enough space to get her hands on my shoulders to turn me around to face her. She had not lost any strength to diabetes or old age, I can tell you that.

"It's okay, honey," she said, her Eastern European accent coming out thick for condolences. "I thought you knew. I thought your sister told you," she revealed, explaining herself and her angry phone call.

"My sister?" I had asked. It was only half a question. I couldn't utter the rest of it.

"When your mother first moved in we exchanged emergency phone numbers. I only had your sister's number," Bella explained. "I began to suspect your mother wasn't skinny from some silly diet so I phoned and phoned her, your sister, but she wouldn't call me back. I finally reached her and told her I thought your mother was sick. She didn't say anything, so I assumed she was very sad, in shock, or something like that. I told her to write down my phone number. When she finally did speak, she said she would be right down. But she never called back and she never came down. Didn't she tell you?"

"No, she didn't," I replied. I couldn't summon up any excuse for her. "Why didn't you call me sooner?" I asked angrily.

"Honey, your mother insisted she was fine and demanded I stay out of her business. I finally took to looking through her things when she was sleeping. I found your name in her address book but the number was written in pencil and it had smudged. I could still make out most of it and kept trying different numbers until I got to you." Bella rubbed her hands up and down my shoulders vigorously, like she was trying to keep my blood circulating.

Then she had pulled me into her abundant chest and guided my head to her shoulder. I had mastered a wealth of intimate positions, but this was not one of them. The basic, comforting hug terrified me. I shored up my defenses and went stiff, steeling my body against the warmth of her body and the burning pain in my throat and chest. It took all the strength I had that

45

Swimming

Naked

day to defend myself against Bella's compliant grandmother's body and her indecipherable words of solace, murmured like a lullaby in her native tongue.

"Okay, here's the deal," my unreliable sister continued into my mother's answering machine. "They want you to come here. George is coming, the girls are coming, and they want you to come."

There was another long pause. She had just told me everything I needed to know. She was back in rehab. I felt not one ounce of pity. In fact, it made me even madder. I imagined her standing at a pay phone at the end of a long hall, tracing diamonds on the floor with her right foot, her left arm remembering some long ago ballet gesture. Her posture would betray her; her back rounded, her chin nearly touching her chest. A nurse would be watching from a respectful but prescribed distance of no more than six feet.

"Lucy, I really fucked up this time," she confessed. I could hear her crying into the phone for what seemed like an eternity.

"Please don't tell Mom," she mumbled, likely cramming her head into her chest, completely dropping the ballerina pretense. "Call Lauren here. She'll tell you."

"She'll tell me my ass," I told the machine. I erased the message and walked down the hall to my mother's room. I sat on the edge of the bed, my knees practically touching her dresser. I looked at all her stuff and wondered when it happened, what was the magic age when women's dressers became tiny little stages filled with the props of an old person. Her room smelled of roses and antiseptic, sweet and cutting at the same time. She must have had eight different brands of perfume, all in their pretty glass bottles on a silver tray I remembered from when it held tiny cut-glass cordial glasses. It was tarnished now and around the base of the perfume bottles were random pills, having fallen out of the ten-plus plastic, amber medicine bottles that shared the silver tray with the perfume.

I had already read all the labels to see if there was anything good left. I was always up for a good prescription sleeping pill or pain reliever. The names of most of my mother's drugs were unrecognizable to me. Her dresser was badly in need of dusting. The dust had congealed on rings of water left when my mother put down her glass, likely after the chill of her nightly martini met the hot Florida night air as she ambled onto the small, narrow veranda off her bedroom. When she came back into her room, she would have to set the glass down on her dresser for a moment to use both hands to pull the sliding door closed. Once she had sealed herself in for the night, she would have likely stabbed out her last cigarette and downed the martini, her "only other vice!" and slowly maneuvered onto the bed.

I pulled my own legs off the floor, slowly, as though I were deeply and secretly in pain. I stared at the ceiling for a long time, wishing I could remember more than one silly prayer. After a while I decided the one I knew would have to do.

I closed my eyes and softly sang, "The Lord is good to me and so I thank the Lord, for giving me the things I need, the sun and the rain and the apple seed. The Lord is good to me."

Swimming

Naked

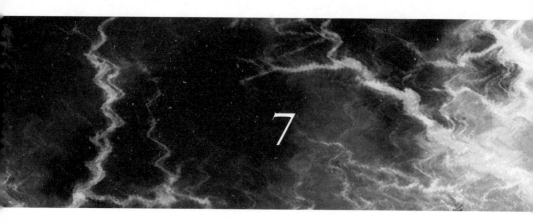

7

"Met your mother and never needed to fly again."

We didn't have many family stories at the time, but that was my father's and he stuck to it. It seemed he could work it into nearly every conversation he had, particularly after two or three of his vacation-sized gin and tonics.

"Met Fay and never needed to fly again," he said, looking into his huge, green plastic tumbler, watching the ice melt. His audience was the boy who cut the grass at the lake, the same boy who was the sole reason for Anna's vacation costume extravaganza and lemonade-serving missions. This boy, Greg, would ride over on his lawn mower, already impressive to my sister and I as we came from a world of push mowers, and drive around our yard, shirtless. My father, who took considerable pride in his own, manual grass-cutting expertise, would mumble over his vacation cocktail ice something about control and a free ride. Greg would mow on heroically, steering with one hand, using the other to wipe sweat off his fore-head, back, or chest. He carried a red bandana for this pur-pose and stuck it into the back pocket of his jeans when he was done mopping himself. Anna would stare at that ban-dana like it was filled with Tom Jones's sweat. She and my mother were in love with Tom Jones. They would both sing "What's New Pussycat?" along with him on the television. It was disgusting.

"Met Fay and never needed to fly again," he told the skinny, greasy attendant at the only gas station near the lake house. I went with him to gas up the car the day before we were leaving to go home. Anna stayed back at the house with my mother, waiting, lemonade in hand, for one final sighting of Greg, the sweating, grass-cutting boy. The gas station was also the store, so I went inside to look at the candy as my dad continued to inform the oil-stained, chipped-tooth gas station kid about his one and only plane trip. It seemed it was the only thing about him that he deemed of interest to anyone else, even though it was hardly interesting and barely made sense.

I thought there were several interesting things about my fa-ther. He should have asked me. He made really good French toast, far better than my mother. She was against soggy bread, period. That's what she said: "I'm against soggy bread." That was as strong a position that she had ever stated about any-thing, so we didn't question her. It sounded impressive.

My dad could pull a quarter from behind my ear then make it disappear again. He would put both of his hands behind his back for a second, and then out they would come, the quarter gone. I would run behind him, looking for the quarter stuck to his sweater. When I came back around to look at his hands again, he would slide one against my head and pick another quarter out of my ear. "Voilà!" he would say. "Voilà!"

He was an excellent driver. That was understood by the whole family. My mother liked to name, title, and register our best and worst traits permanently. There was no room to improve or deteriorate once she had made a decision about our skills and interests.

"Frank is an excellent driver."

"Anna is afraid."

"Lucy is a klutz."

Those were the main things.

My father had a giant hair that grew out of his left eyebrow. His eyebrows were black and bushy to begin with. When he didn't shave in the morning, he looked like an escaped convict, hairy and dark. When he did shave, he looked very handsome, even in his tan work overalls. His hair would be dark and wet from the shower and he smelled of baby powder in a doctor's office. This is how he looked every Monday through Friday morning on his way to work. It was the only time I ever saw him kiss my mother. She would be at the sink, doing the dishes. He would walk past Anna and me at the kitchen table and wink at us. Then he would come up behind my mother, put his arms around her waist, and squeeze tight while he kissed her on the neck, always the left side. Depending upon her mood, she would either squeal, girlishly, then wriggle, playfully, and swat him away or go completely rigid, not moving an inch or washing one single dish until he let go.

Her response never seemed to matter to my father. He would walk to the back door and turn, smiling. He would grab the bill of his work cap, tilt his head toward us, and say, "Good day, ladies."

We would just stare at him, silent, then return to our morning activity as soon as he left. It was a woman's household. I heard my mother tell her sister he was like an appliance. "He's necessary, all right, just a little noisy sometimes," she laughed into the phone as though this was the funniest joke in the world, blowing billows of cigarette smoke around the kitchen.

I watched his lips moving and I began silently telling his story, my lips moving along with his. I couldn't hear him, all the way inside the store. But I could hear him inside my head. "I wasn't much of a salesman, that's for sure, but they needed someone to go to St. Louis and man the booth at the trade show. That was in 1961." He always put a lot of emphasis on the date. "Nineteen SIX-TEE-one," then he would pause dramatically.

He would tell the boy filling our car with gas that he didn't sell a single press while he was there. He would repeat that he is not a salesman. He's a machinist. And a good one. He would let on that he didn't speak to more than three people in all four days of the show. That he sat at the table and spread out the J.P. Printing Press brochures in front of him, fanning them like he had seen at the other booths and tables. But he didn't speak to a single person the whole time. He didn't want to come across too pushy.

My dad was leaning up against the back of the car, tilting his head back so his face was in the sun. He had his arms crossed, so when he took a deep breath his arms would rise up along with his chest. The gas station boy never took his eyes off the clicking, rolling numbers on the gas pump. He stared at the numbers and ran his tongue in and out of the gap in his teeth, his lips snarled like he was remembering the taste of something bitter and bad. Without looking back, he began to pull the gas nozzle out of the car, his eyes still intently focused on what would be the final number on the pump, his tongue on the raggedy tooth. I saw my father turn toward the boy and clap his hands together, signaling he was coming to the end of his tale.

"I didn't think much about the trade show one way or the other until I called back to the plant on my last day in St. Louis. Stan, my boss, was not happy one bit to hear I didn't have a single lead. He said, 'I knew I should have sent Ken,' and hung up the phone."

My father followed the boy into the store to finish his story and to pay for the gas. I was trying to get his attention by pulling on his arm, then his pockets, then his whole leg. I was invisible to him. He had to finish it now, regardless of whether anyone was listening.

"Now, I'm not one to worry, but I was pretty much bothered by the time I got on that plane to go back home. I was sitting next to the window, looking out at the wing, wondering if they could actually fire me for not handing out the brochures. The next thing I heard was a voice saying, 'Well, don't you look like you need a drink?' "

This was the only part of the story I liked. I loved to think of my mother as he saw her. It made her more interesting. She was a woman with a past.

"I looked up and saw Fay. She had her hair up the way she wears it. She had a tiny bit of bright red lipstick on her front tooth. She was wearing the tightest, blue stewardess uniform I had ever seen with the shiniest set of wings pinned to her chest. I loved her the minute I saw her and married her two weeks later. Yep. After I met Fay, I never needed to fly again."

"I thought you got to fly for free if you were married to a stewardess," said the boy as he was fishing through the change in the drawer.

My father and I both looked at him, startled. He had been listening, apparently, which wasn't how this usually played out. "Huh, you don't say?" or "That's nice" were typical sorts of responses. Greg the grass cutter had just nodded his head, like he was trying to be polite, but he hadn't really been listening at all.

"She quit her job the day we were married," my father countered, a bit indignant, as though the idea of it, him flying for free or her still flying the friendly skies after they were married, did not make sense at all.

"Oh," the boy mumbled, handing over my father's change. He handed me a piece of bubble gum and smiled. He was full of surprises, this one.

We drove back in silence. I was putting holes in the bubble gum with my tongue when it started to rain. We were pulling in from the road to our hidden driveway. I prayed it would just be a rainstorm and that it would rain very, very softly, but it started to get heavier and heavier and louder and louder as we drove down the long gravel driveway. Even underneath all the trees in the heaviest part of the woods between the main road and our house, my father had to turn the windshield wipers to their fastest speed.

As we pulled into the grass clearing, the first crack of thunder shook the car. The sky had become almost as dark as night. I could see my mother grabbing towels off the line as fast as she could. When she pulled down the last one, a giant striped beach towel, I saw Greg and Anna, revealed as though the curtain had just gone up on their play. Anna was wearing my mother's pink and lacy short nightgown. On Anna, it dragged the ground unless she tied it up at the waist with something. I could see she had tethered herself with a jump rope. She wore her green bathing suit under the slip and had fashioned a wrist corsage out of red plastic flowers and some pipe cleaner.

A flash of lightning illuminated the scene, appearing to immobilize everyone in the spotlight. Greg was caught wiping his forehead with his bandanna, this time soaking up rain, not sweat; my mother was running up the wooden steps to the porch, holding a bundle of towels in one arm and the striped beach towel over her head with the other. Anna appeared with her arms outstretched, holding a near-empty glass of lemonade. She was turned toward the house, frozen, as though a bullet to the back was about to throw her tiny, arched body into the air. I closed my eyes. When I opened them, Anna was falling into the beach towel held by my mother at the top of the stairs. My mother was motioning for Greg to come into the house.

"Oh boy," my father sighed, moving the gearshift into park. He turned off the ignition and lit a cigarette and sat staring at the house. I sat next to him, staring too. We stayed that way, silent. I chewed my gum in rhythm to the windshield wipers as my father's smoke began to fill the car and fog the windows. The rain pounded out a warning on the metal roof of the station wagon. My father used his forearm to wipe a patch of fog away. We kept staring at the house until the patch fogged over again. When it became clear that the storm wasn't going to let up outside, we knew we had to make a run for it and face my sister, the real tempest, inside.

8

"THE CONTEMPORARY!" Someone I didn't recognize answered the phone with this perky new institutional name and zippy attitude that clearly came out of some four-hour brainstorming session with that moronic marketing committee.

I asked the phone-answering person to put me through to the director.

"May I tell him who is calling?"

"It's Lucy Greene."

I might as well have said Cruella De Vil.

"Oh, umm, hi, umm, hold on." I was put on hold by this now befuddled young woman.

"Ms. Greene?" She was back on the line.

"Yes?" I asked.

"You have a lot of messages and packages and faxes. A lot," she emphasized.

"Did they tell you why I am away?" I asked her.

"Oh, yes, well, yes. I'm sorry. I tell them you have a family emergency. Some of them still insist on speaking to you. Some people get really angry that they haven't heard from you," she quickly explained, relieved to be unloading the anxiety of what she believed to be unfairly in her camp back to where she felt it belonged: with me, leaning against the wall, talking on a pay phone in the Boca Siesta Memorial Hospital lobby, my mother glassy-eyed and disoriented, picking invisible bugs off her scrawny arms, right down the hall.

"May I speak with Patrick? Is he in?" ignoring the package of stress she was trying to deliver to me.

"What should I do with—"

"May I speak with Patrick!" I demanded, cutting her off and taking full advantage of my reputation as a bitch.

I traced the lines around the painted concrete blocks on the wall as I waited to be put through to Patrick. I could see him walking slowly down the hall to his office. There was little that could hurry that man. He would stop and ask his secretary for a cup of coffee, putting his hand on her shoulder and asking in a way that said he realized this was a very big favor in this day when secretaries just didn't fetch coffee. She got him coffee three times a day, every day. And every single time he asked her as though he had never made this request before and never would again. She adored him. We all adored him.

He would move past Clara's desk. She took care of membership, what little there was of it to take care of. "Remind me to tell you about a nifty little reciprocal membership I drummed up for us with my old friend Jack Stilton."

Patrick came from the old school of museum management, which meant there was not a lot of visible management going on, but there were a lot of phone calls to other museum directors and trips to other museums to meet with other directors. At first it all appeared to be the duties of what looked to be a very cushy job. Call a buddy, go to Europe to see said buddy, the wife and kids meeting up for a bit of a holiday in, say, the south of France.

But I also came to appreciate that my best curatorial efforts, regardless of how well conceived and important, weren't worth shit when it came to getting someone to call me back from a gallery in New York. Patrick would read one of my proposals, lean back in his chair, and stare dreamily at the ceiling. He would say, "You know who would be good for this show? Liskey," having just named the hot photographer of the moment. "Do you want me to call him?"

"Lucy?" he answered.

"Hola!" I replied.

"How are you?" he asked. I could imagine him settling into his chair. Picking up a stack of mail from the in-box on the corner of his desk.

"Well . . . ," I began, ready to launch into a stand-up routine of cold, calculated hospital jokes and witty, caustic observations about the nurses, doctors, my dying mother. When I got nervous, no one was spared. But I couldn't speak. If I did I would cry. I could barely get out "sorry."

"Oh, Lucy," Patrick said. "Are you down there all by your-self?" he asked.

"Yep," I croaked.

"What about your sister? Did she find you? She called for you here several times so I finally took the call. She was very concerned. I told her I thought your mother was ill, but I didn't tell her how sick she was," he recounted. "She said she was going to get her things packed and get on the next plane."

There's nothing like the taste of fury to overcome despondency.

"Oh, she ran into some problems herself," I told him. We used our secrets as weapons for destruction within the family compound only, keeping them close like cyanide pills.

"So what's going on there?" I asked, diverting attention away from the real issues at hand. "That new girl is disgustingly cheerful. Did she tour with Up with People?"

"Hmm," mumbled Patrick. I would have bet money he was reading his mail.

"She says there are a lot of messages for me," I said.

"Oh, yes, there are a lot of messages for you," Patrick responded, repeating pretty much exactly what I had said to give himself time to focus back on me and away from whatever else had distracted him. He was a very clever nonlistener.

"Don't worry, Lucy. And don't bother to call in unless you need to talk. Everything here is as urgent as you want it to be. You could be on the phone for three hours a day or you could never call in for two months. Everything will come out pretty much the same. It's up to you," he coached. "The art world was around a pretty long time before you came along to shake it up. I'm pretty sure it will be here when you get back," he teased.

I was about to respond in some smart-ass way when he said, "My mother died of cancer, you know."

"I didn't know that, Patrick. I'm sorry," I said nervously. I was afraid to hear more. I hated it when people revealed themselves to me directly, with words. I liked it when artists revealed themselves through a painting or an object or a photograph, the medium as a medium. I could take all sorts of pain and misery, one step removed. But this wasn't easy territory for Patrick either. He had made tiptoeing on the sharp edges of existence his life's work.

"Were you and your mother close?" Patrick asked. "I don't recall you speaking much about her or your family." He must have been wearing protective boots today.

"Yes . . . well . . . no," I began, stumbling for the exact nature of our relationship. "I mean, she is my mom."

"I'll bet she's got a few stories to tell," Patrick mused, chuckling.

"I have no idea," I confessed, rubbing my temple. I was dying for a drink of water.

"That photographer, Kyle McDaniels, dropped off a package for you," he said cheerfully, happy to change the subject. "Well, actually it's two packages. One is of his recent work. The trees. The other package he wanted us to send to you. He seemed very eager for you to have it."

"You don't say," I said, clever in my own way with non-committal responses.

"He's very good," Patrick praised. "I would like to show this work. Have you seen it?"

"No, I haven't seen it." I wanted to make some joke but I couldn't think. I suddenly wished for my own morphine drip. My ears were hot.

"I'm going to send both of these packages to you," Patrick decided. "We have your mother's address, don't we?" "We" meant Jan, his secretary.

"I don't know, let me talk to Jan." I was eager to conclude this call. There was way too much information coming my way and I was suddenly feeling a little ill.

"Take care of yourself, Lucy. Take as much time as you need," Patrick encouraged.

I gave my mother's address to Jan and begged off quickly, claiming I had to go meet with the doctors.

"Fuck, fuck, fuck," I whispered to myself, walking down the hall toward my mother's room. I turned around and headed back the way I came, past the phone, past the ambulance unloading someone for a visit to the emergency room, past the parking lot, past the three-story medical building next door, past the little park, past the doughnut shop. I came to the largest intersection in Boca Siesta. My heart was pounding so fast I thought I might be having a heart attack. I couldn't see straight or hear right. I was on the run and I had nowhere to go. I was alternately afraid of shitting myself and stepping in front of a passing car. I wanted to lie on the ground. I wanted to wrap my arms around the base of a tree. I wanted to throw up. I wanted a cigarette but was sure that would make my heart race even faster. I was certain I was losing my mind.

I started bouncing up and down like a jogger who can't stay still for even one second at a traffic light. I clapped my hands over my head, behind my back, in front of me, jumping up and down. I kept the rhythm by chanting, "Fuck, fuck, fuck, fuck, fuck."

Once I had jumped myself out of the feeling of imminent, terrifying danger and insanity, I began to walk back toward the hospital. I was exhausted. I stopped to sit on a bench in the park. I put my head in my hands and started to cry. It lasted only a minute.

I sat up and pulled the neck of my T-shirt up to wipe the tears off my face. I pulled out my cigarettes and lit one, inhaling deeply. I watched as a remarkably old and feeble woman pushed an equally old and feeble man in a wheelchair past me, heading back to the hospital, I guessed. I wondered for a moment how she did it; how she took care of him when she could barely walk herself. She looked my way and smiled.

I looked down at the ground and remembered I had to ask the nurse to ask the doctor about my mother's medications. I flicked my cigarette behind me and headed for the hospital, overtaking the elderly woman and her charge in four long, easy strides. I never once looked back.

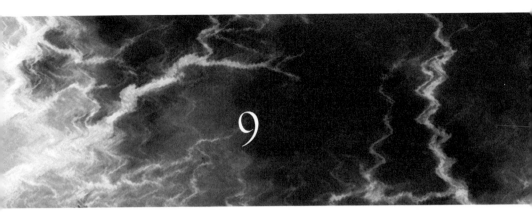

9

We made a run for it. When we reached the screened-in porch, we were as wet as though we had just gone swimming in the lake. My mother had put a stack of beach towels on the wooden table, along with neat stacks of sheets and pillowcases in preparation for the ritual packing of the car. My father tossed me a towel and began to dry himself off with another from the stack. We could hear Anna screaming from somewhere inside the house.

My mother came out on the porch, turning on the overhead light while simultaneously slamming the screen door. It was as effective as lightning and thunder. We stood at attention.

She barked, "Those towels are clean!"

My father and I remained totally still. He looked straight at her. I looked straight at the ground. We had come to know, somehow, that if we didn't move or talk back, she might move on, just like a wasp.

She made a sound of sheer exasperation and went back into the house. We started to move again, slowly, drying ourselves off. We were startled when the door squeaked open again and so we froze, like we were playing a game.

"You still need to pack the car tonight," she told my father, as though the storm, Anna, her dark mood were all his fault. It was a ridiculous request. But Anna's screams were a reminder to both of us that however you might manage it, it would probably be better to be outside the house in the storm than inside with my sister.

My sister was pretty much afraid of everything, but she was absolutely terrified of storms. She was afraid of loud noises, crowds of people, the dark, and being alone, to name a few. When confronted by one of the more minor scary things, Anna's white skin would become even whiter, her eyes would go wide, and her whole body would freeze. If you watched her closely, you could see she was trembling slightly, like there was a tiny earthquake in her belly. It would look as though she wasn't even breathing.

"Lucy, you had better go inside and help your mother," he said quietly. He took his towel and began to dry my hair, first with rough-and-tumble moves that felt like punishment, then with slow, soft strokes that felt like love.

We both knew what he was sending me into. It would have been hard to say who had gotten the worst job between the two of us. I left his warm hands and went inside, closing the porch door behind me as quietly as I could. I looked back and saw my father standing with our two wet towels in his hands, trying to figure out what my mother would deem the proper thing to do with them. I pressed my face up against the tiny holes in the grid of the screen and watched him fold one into a tidy square and place it on the pile with the other towels. He shook out the other and draped it over the back of the wobbly rocking chair. For a moment, he held on to the back of the chair, one hand on each side of the tall back, like he was holding a friend steady. He tucked his chin to his chest, then tilted his head way back, looking up at the ceiling. I could see the rise and fall of his chest as he took two deep breaths. He slowly tipped his head forward until he was staring straight ahead.

He suddenly looked like an old man to me, his legs sad and hairy under his long shorts, his belly sticking out past his chest under his wet, striped T-shirt. He picked up the stack of towels, kicked the porch door open, and went down the steps into the dark of the driving rain. I turned around and pressed my back up against the door. I tucked my chin into my chest and then tilted my head back just like my father had done. I took my own deep breath and snapped my head forward. I walked toward the kitchen, where I could hear my mother slamming things around and Anna wailing. I moved fast so I wouldn't lose my nerve.

Greg was sitting in a chair at the far end of the living room. He was staring down at his lap. I had no use for him when he was cutting the grass or sweating in our yard, and I certainly had no use for him now. I gave him a look in which I tried to convey my disinterest, but he never once looked up. I moved through the dining room toward the din of my sister and my mother.

The kitchen was huge, by my standards. In the cooking part were two long walls with open cabinets and shiny, speckled countertops that intersected at two sinks in the corner of the room. The refrigerator was at the end of one of the rows of cabinets and countertops, closest to the eating part of the kitchen, where a round wooden table surrounded by six chairs sat next to the window, facing the back of the house. The stove was by the door that led to the dining room, where I was standing. In the middle of the room, between the stove and the refrigerator, was an island. My mother loved this invention and spoke of it all year round.

"If I had an island I could really do some cooking," she would say yearningly back home, chopping vegetables on the small space of the counter between the refrigerator and the sink, her arms pressed tightly to her sides. "There is no room!" she would shout, disgusted, holding a bunch of cut-up celery in her hands, with nowhere to go with the small green pieces except the sink, the garbage can, or the pot on the stove.

"They'll just have to cook with everything else," she would declare, finishing, "oh, well." The way my mother said it, "oh, well" meant the meal was basically ruined now.

I couldn't see Anna when I first came into the kitchen, but I knew exactly where she was. My mother was reaching on top of the refrigerator to pull down our cereal boxes. I came around the island, which had been blocking my view of the floor, and saw Anna, with her arms wrapped around my mother's leg, her left cheek pressed against the back of my mother's calf. She had her eyes closed tight but the tears were streaming out of them anyway, leaking out from all sides. My mother was attempting to pack up the kitchen, dragging her hysterical daughter around the floor as she went, like a pirate with a heavy wooden leg.

"Take this box out to the porch," she instructed me, pointing to one of the three boxes on top of the island. I looked at her without moving.

"Now!" she shouted, making Anna cry even harder. I couldn't reach the box on the counter, and she made no move to indicate she understood that. I knew she was a bit handicapped with Anna attached to her leg, but that didn't help me to know how to get the box down. I reached up with one hand, stretching as much as I could. I could feel the side of the box with my fingertips and so I started to slide it across the top of the island.

"What in the hell are you doing?" my mother asked, indignant.

"I can't reach," I explained.

My sister had pulled my mother's leg into an unnatural position far behind her body. She looked back at Anna with sheer hate in her eyes and wrenched her leg free from her grip, in one fast and powerful move. Anna wasn't fast enough to catch herself. Her head slammed onto the kitchen floor and she began to cry without making a sound, which was a very bad sign. It meant the worst kind of crying was about to begin.

My mother had had it. She picked my sister up from behind, lifting her by her armpits, and pulled her into the dining room, shuffling her feet and dragging her like a corpse.

"Come watch your sister," she snapped at me. I would rather have taken the boxes to the porch, but I kept quiet and followed my mother and Anna into the living room.

My mother dumped my sister on the braided rag rug in front of the dingy, yellow couch. The coffee table was still off to the side where my dad had moved it the night before. Anna had wanted to show me a dance she had made up. There was never enough room for her dance routines. Greg was still sitting in the chair, staring at his thighs under his wet pants. We ignored him and he us.

"Anna, get up on the couch and I'll cover you up with a blanket," my mother coaxed, trying to get Anna calmed down enough to resume breathing. "You too, Lucy. Up on the couch." I hopped up onto the couch fast. I knew my part.

My mother grabbed a blanket from the wooden chest next to the bookcase and came over to me on the couch, pretending to ignore my sister for a minute.

"There you go, Lucy," she cooed, tucking the blanket up under my chin and rubbing my forehead. My mother's most tender moments with me were devices to lure my sister up and out of some misery. I was merely the decoy.

Anna wasn't budging this time. She had gone rigid, her legs out in front of her and her back as straight as a board. She had gotten herself into such an extreme state of hysteria that her body was resisting her need to breathe. This made her even more panicked and she began to kick her feet against the floor. My mother picked her up again and dropped her on the couch. This seemed to work. Anna took in a huge gulp of air, and then several more, ragged, weeping ones, finally letting out a wail. That was part of the cycle. If she could breathe, she could also scream.

My father came into the room from the porch, dripping wet. My mother turned toward him. She started to yell at him for being wet in the house but was too exhausted to muster up any more irrational rage. Instead, she began to cry herself and marched out of the room and back toward the kitchen. She returned immediately with one of the packed boxes. She dropped it at my father's feet and said, "Here." She went back for another box, crying all the way. Anna got up off the couch and ran to my father, wrapping herself around both of his legs. I stayed still on the couch, pulling the blanket up over my nose.

"Would you like me to help you?" came a muffled voice from the corner. It startled all of us. We weren't used to witnesses.

"I don't mind the rain," Greg said, standing up.

Anna looked up at him from her beggar's position on the floor, where she remained attached to my father's legs. It suddenly seemed to occur to her that this boy had watched her in all of her agony. Now she was both agonized and humiliated, so she began to cry even louder. She let go of my father and came back toward me. She viciously grabbed the blanket out of my hands and fell into the other end of the couch, her face buried and her body heaving.

As Greg and my father began to pick up the boxes and bags my mother had been dropping by the door, the storm dropped a few more loud hints that it wasn't even close to being over. I realized I had been left alone, once again, to watch my sister fall apart.

I was pondering how I might best console my sister when the lights went out, sending my sister into an almost unimaginable state of panic. She started pounding the back of the couch with both of her fists, in an absolute rage over her misfortune.

"Fuck," my mother swore, dropping a box on the floor.

I spun around to look at her as she walked back into the darkness toward the kitchen. I had never heard her say that word before. It was hard to figure out where to focus. The drama was unfolding all over the place. I don't think Anna heard a word. She began to cry in dry heaves again, not breathing. She was kneeling on the couch facing the window, hammering out her anger with her fists in rhythmic bursts. I looked outside. A flash of lightning revealed Greg handing a soaked box to my father, who was trying to quickly cram it into the station wagon. My father's head was inside the wagon. He motioned with his arm for Greg to go back inside the house. Greg turned to come back in and looked at us in the window. Seeing him looking up at her was just too much for Anna to bear. She bent her head over the back of the couch and threw up.

"Mom, Anna threw up!" I reported, looking over the back of the couch onto the floor where the mess was. It was a huge mess of a mess too. I remembered we ate hot dogs for lunch and almost threw up myself.

"Mom!" I yelled again, "Anna threw—"

"I heard you the first time!" my mother interrupted, suddenly standing right behind me.

"Where?" she asked.

"Back there," I said, pointing behind the couch.

She moved behind Anna and squatted down beside the couch, dragging the whole side of it toward the center of the room, away from Anna's vomit. I was bent over the back of the couch looking at the grossness on the floor when I felt the lightning strike. It was so close to the house it simultaneously lit up and shook the whole room. I looked at Anna to see what this would do to her, as though everything wasn't already bad enough. She had stopped crying. She was staring out the window, completely motionless. I thought she had run out of fluid in her body, having either cried it out or thrown it up. I looked outside where she was looking and I saw it; the thing that was beyond any terror Anna could concoct for herself. My father was lying on the ground far from the station wagon, near the base of the dead tree with the tire swing, smoke pouring out of his body. The storm had reached out and smacked my father. The lightning must have wrapped its long, electric fingers around him and hurled him to the ground.

10

She awoke with a start and sat straight up in bed.

"Lucy? Wake up. I have thought of something important and I want you to write it down," she commanded, with fairly convincing authority, considering the morphine.

I was awake already. I had been staring at the way the light snuck through the blinds, even when they were in their clenched, closed position. I stood up and bent over in a futile attempt to touch my toes. My body was beginning to surrender into a lazy, cramped ball of spongy, tired flesh. When I stood back up, I was light-headed. I put my hand on my mother's bed to balance myself.

"Remember those red squares we crocheted? All those squares we made with that tiny, little loom? Give those to your sister. I still have them. She could make a wonderful blanket with them. It will be nice for her to have that, at least. I am sure she still sews beautifully."

"Oh, how perfect," I thought. Anna can't hold her forty-dollar wineglass anymore without shaking the expensive French wine right out of it. I'm sure some delicate handwork will be a great thing for her palsied, alcoholic hands.

"Oh, she'll like that!" I said. "I'll look for them tonight."

Our exchanges, my mother's and mine, albeit few and far between, were generally of this nature. Some days she would be relatively lucid, others a mush-mouthed dope head. Articulate or not, her comments seemed to be a mental inventory of every "to do" list she had ever written or considered. She was specifically concerned with every task that remained unfinished. It seemed to me that these tasks, the undone ones, were never completed because they were never important to begin with.

Thus, I had given up on the notion that my mother would suddenly adopt some deeply held life-and-death philosophy and pass away with a martyr's conviction of something, anything, profound. She just wanted to clean the slate, to do her chores. There are no weekend seminars for spirituality or Cliffs Notes for Christianity, Judaism, or Buddhism. This was the business of a life's journey and my mother's trip had been cut short. To further complicate matters, she never even realized she had been traveling.

I put my hand on hers, briefly. I thought she was fading off, back into a fitful sleep. But she rallied, struggling to sit back up. She was eager to check a few more things off her list.

"My car still runs. Well, you know that, you've been driving it. I don't know why you rented a car in the first place.

Anyway, you should have George drive it up to Cincinnati for one of the girls."

This car, which George the neurosurgeon was supposed to drive more than a thousand miles back to his million-dollar home, to park in his four-car garage next to his Mercedes, was a giant boat of a falling-apart Ford, a luxury sedan in a former life, that would totally mortify these two privileged, privately schooled, and, frankly, very prissy girls. Precociousness is a precarious attribute for children. One day you wake up and you are detestable for doing or saying the very thing that was darling the day before. That day had come and gone for both Sarah Elizabeth, nearly ten, and her little sister, Maura Francine, eight.

"Okay. I'll give him a call."

"You should take it in for a tune-up this week, you know," she instructed. "They can tell you where to take it at the gatehouse.

"And there is one other thing," she said primly, studying her fingernails as though there were something there to look at besides brittle, chalky white stubs. She sat there, frozen. I thought she had gotten lost in a druggy haze like a pot smoker, diverted midsentence in the study of a speck of dust falling through space, backlit by the sun.

I assumed that was it for our conversation. I turned around and walked to the window and began to slowly rotate the thin rod in my fingers to let a little more sun through the horizontal slats of the blinds.

74

"Lucy, I know where your father is. I think you should see him."

I spun back around to look at her, expecting her to be lying on her bed, her eyes half shut, these words delivered in a delirium.

She was sitting up, her hands posed as though her nails were still wet from a manicure. She was staring at me with such cold, ice blue clarity in her eyes it slowly began to register that she was telling me the truth.

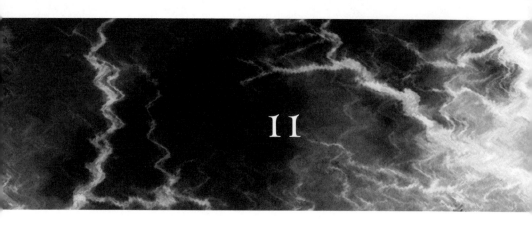

II

"Anna, let me in," I said, loud enough to be heard by Anna through our locked bedroom door and quiet enough so that I wouldn't wake up my mother, who was napping again. It didn't matter if my father heard me or not.

"Let me in!" I repeated in a stage whisper. There was no keyhole so I decided to lie down with my face pressed against the gray, scratchy wall-to-wall carpet to try to look under the door. I wanted to look at the wallpaper books again. My mother had decided we needed to "freshen things up!" So yesterday, in between her naps, she went to the wallpaper store and brought home three huge books filled with wallpaper samples. Each book had a handle on the side and you carried them like you would a suitcase. They were so heavy; Anna and I had to drag them up the stairs. She took two and I took one.

When we got them into our room, we heaved them onto Anna's bed and began to look through them, one at a time.

Each page was big and heavy and smelled like glue. Every time we turned a page it sounded like sneakers in the rain and looked like the future. Anna was trying to decide if the future should cover the walls with ladies in frilly dresses holding pink parasols or with mod, purple, flower-power designs. I was leaning more toward bright blue and yellow stripes, the blue stripe fat and the yellow stripe thin. There was a whole book called "Mix and Match," where you were supposed to use two different wallpapers in one room. My mother thought this was a great idea, one wallpaper for me and one for Anna. Although in the end, I knew Anna would pick out what she wanted and the two of them would claim that I had chosen some dizzying red-and-pink pattern of seashells.

We did agree on one thing. Every time we turned those loud pages of the books and came upon anything that remotely resembled the thing on my father's back, we turned the page fast. If we could have torn those pages out, we would have. Instead, we moved as quickly as we could past ferns and trees. Neither of us had to say anything. It was weird enough just thinking about it. Living with it was another story.

It was practically impossible to pretend that nothing had happened at the lake, with my father stumbling around the house like he was retarded, picking at his clothes. He hardly talked at all, but when he did he said his clothes hurt. We came to believe that meant his clothes hurt his skin. My mother insisted that he wear pants, or at least his pajama bottoms, but let him go around without a shirt. When he ran into Anna or me, which we tried to avoid at all times, he would pet us like we were dogs, not children; patting one, two, three times on the tops of our heads. My mother took on the look of an insane person. We had seen such people on television. You knew they were crazy because of the way their eyes darted back and forth.

She would come into our room, smile, her eyes jumping from me to Anna back to me then back to Anna, then over to the window, then back to Anna. She would say "okay" like she had found everything, including us, to be in order. Then she would leave. If her door was closed, that meant she was napping. It was closed almost all the time.

The door to our bedroom suddenly swung open and I was looking straight up at my sister, who appeared huge and scary to me. Her eyes darted about too, only she was looking up and down the hall and at me in between.

"Why didn't you let me in?" I asked.

"None of your business, stupid," she responded. She stepped over me and walked down the hall, past my mother's closed door, and started down the stairs.

"Wait up!" I called after her as I got up off the floor. I could see her head disappearing down the stairs. She wasn't very good company but she was better than no company. I ran toward the stairs, slowing for quiet steps outside the door where my mother was sleeping.

Anna was pushing open the screen door when I got to the bottom of the stairs. She looked back at me for a second then went on outside, letting the door slam behind her. The part of the door that used to stop it midslam and ease it into its frame had been broken for a couple of weeks. My dad could barely feed himself without slopping food all over the place, so he wasn't going to fix it. And all the people who turned up after the lightning struck him had quit coming around.

"Well, everything seems pretty much back to normal," I had heard my aunt Sally say as she zipped up her giant, black purse. My mother was leaning against the kitchen counter, smoking her tenth cigarette in as many minutes. My father was eating cereal, letting the milk spill out of his mouth and roll down his chin, his neck, and onto his naked chest. Sally was the last one to leave.

"Why don't you girls come visit me?" she asked, leaning down to kiss us good-bye, outside by her car. Anna started crying and wrapped herself around my mother's legs.

"Can we go inside?" she begged my mother.

"I'll come," I said to Aunt Sally and proceeded to get in her car. I was ready to leave at any time, no bags necessary. My mother laughed and tried to pull me out of the backseat. I went limp so she really had to work at it. My mother gave me a look that I hadn't seen before as her sister drove away. She looked to be considering something very important. I thought for a second she was going to say something, but she picked up my sister, who was far too big to be carried, and lugged her inside the house instead. And that's pretty much where we all stayed for the rest of the summer. Outside was not someplace any of us, except my father, really wanted to be.

I opened the screen door and headed down the steps to the backyard. I couldn't believe Anna was outside at all. It wasn't storming or anything, but still, she had been in the house for weeks. She was standing behind my father with her arms crossed. She looked mad. I came up and stood beside her.

He was sitting in a lawn chair with his feet in our wading pool. He had on his pajama bottoms but he hadn't rolled them up, so the cuffs were floating on top of the water, along with a bunch of tiny pieces of grass, thrown there by a regular push model of a mower over a month ago, when my father cut our grass for the last time. He was hunched over with his arms limp at his sides. His head was down and his eyes were closed.

We stared at his back for a long time. The thing should have been gone by now. It had a name, a real medical name, but we just called it the thing. It looked like the lightning that struck my father had gotten stuck underneath his skin. Or like a tree in the winter, with all its bare, twisted branches, had been tattooed on his back. Its trunk started low and on the left, almost on his side, then grew up toward the center of his back, with all of its branches nearly covering him. It reached all the way up to his neck.

"This is really strange," the doctor said the last time he came to the house, as though that thing on my dad's back was the only strange thing he noticed. He hadn't mentioned the plates stacked up on both sides of the sink, or that my mother was using a can of tuna with tuna in it for an ashtray. Or that my sister was wearing her raincoat and her rain boots, plus gloves and a hat and a scarf, and it was summer and she was indoors.

"I hate you," Anna told the thing on our father's back, or our father. I wasn't sure which. She was still wearing the raincoat and boots but had left the other winter gear inside. She pulled up the hood on her coat and said it again. "I hate you."

I tried to move forward to see her face around the hood. My foot got caught up on the hose that was lying by the pool and I started to fall. I stuck my hand out to catch myself. I got my balance and looked to see how. My hand was resting palm down, wide open on my father's back, my fingers becoming a part of the thing's strange pattern. I looked at Anna, keeping my hand on his back. She looked deadly serious. She was staring at my hand. I looked back at it and the thing underneath. I was studying it all, my hand, the figure, my father's back, when my sister's hand appeared on top of mine.

We stood like that for a long time, my father leaning over the edge of our tiny pool, my hand on his back and Anna's on mine.

Swimming

Naked

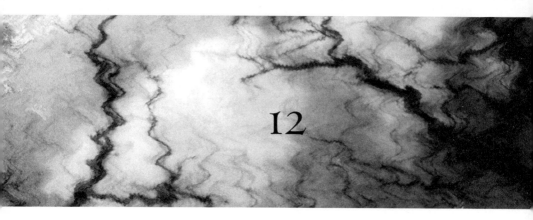

12

I WAS SITTING in the cafeteria drinking a cup of coffee. I was trying to ascertain whether the coffee was just plain bad or if the Styrofoam cup was informing the taste of the beverage. I had entered a totally different world and this was exactly the sort of thing I found myself considering as if it were a topic for serious curatorial study in this strange, vacuous realm.

The hospital was like its own weird space city. Once inside the complex, time was measured by shift changes, meals, doctor's rotations, and tests, not by the morning sun, the end of a workday, the evening meal. I could watch the rest of the world on the omnipresent glowing and murmuring television sets, but it felt like I was peeking in on the fodder of Planet Earth, some faraway land of the living. These alien creatures could be terribly amusing; their fears, their battles, their sports, their chair-throwing tantrums with their new, proud ghetto language. I felt completely removed from the "normal" world.

I didn't even feel close to the task at hand. I was watching my mother die like I was watching myself watch my mother die, hovering just out of harm's way, an apathetic angel in my own protective space suit.

To be fair, this ability to disconnect, this propensity to float and observe and detach, has been previously noted, by former lovers in general and more specifically by my therapist.

"You just disappeared," one man cleverly observed after I left him at a bar, ordering me another drink, while I went to the bathroom. I had looked in the mirror at my half-drunk self and decided it was time to go home. I was bored, so I left.

"Sometimes I think you're not really listening to me," another lover remarked, after droning on about an ex-girlfriend or some other silly topic.

"There is some cold blood running through those veins of yours," the last one mentioned, while tying up the laces on his boots, sitting on the few things I had laid out on my bed to pack for Florida. His name is Kyle and he's a photographer who just moved to Cleveland. I moved fast to get him into my bed because he was brilliant and quiet and hot, literally. The first time I met him I could feel the heat rising up out of his body, like a fever. I came to believe that this palpable warmth was the result of his considerable depth of field, emotionally. He was the first person I had ever met who didn't feel like an abstraction to me. His boundaries were totally clear. If I crossed a line, I could feel the heat. It warned and beckoned. He terrified me.

"What are you protecting yourself from?" my therapist asked. "What are you most afraid of?"

"Duh," I thought. "Intimacy, I guess," I mumbled, slumped down in my chair.

It was clear I had issues. But I had an ace in the hole when it came to my problems. I used it like a winning hand of poker, keeping it close to the vest while I listened to the other players of my generation.

"I've been on Prozac for two years now. It helps take the edge off when I'm really stressed out." This was confided to me by a surgeon and trustee on the museum board, who worked seventy-five hours a week and cheated on his wife and occasionally indulged in other, more uplifting pharmaceuticals, stolen from the hospital where he worked.

"I take Ritalin. It helps me concentrate," explained the museum's registrar, her anal-retentiveness fueled by this nirvana for the obsessive-compulsive adult.

"I'm just sad," my next-door neighbor confessed, crying inconsolably on the couch in my apartment, pulling wads of tissues out of her Gucci handbag. "I've always gotten everything I wanted and now I don't want any of it," she wept.

Sometimes I would keep my hand concealed. Other times I would start spreading out the cards, one at a time, to the stunned amazement of my audience.

"When I was six my father was struck by lightning," I would begin. That would get them every time.

84

"My sister saw the whole thing. I was right next to her,"

I would explain, laying down the next card. "We were on vacation. I just wasn't looking out the window at that very moment."

"Did he die?" was usually the first question.

"No, he suffered serious neurological damage and became a lightning celebrity of sorts," I illuminated, assuming my educator's voice, conducting a little tour through my family's gallery of curiosities. "There are these patterns that appear on some victims of massive electrical shock. They're known as Lichtenberg figures because of their similarity to the patterns described by Georg Lichtenberg, some German physicist, who found the same patterns when he was experimenting with static electricity, the first copy machines, actually. My dad's figure looked like he had a bolt of lightning or a barren tree tattooed on his back. The figures are supposed to disappear after a day or two. Only my dad's stayed."

I would pause before laying down the final card, the ace of hearts of my royal personal history flush. "It was my dad who disappeared. My sister and I woke up one morning a couple of months after the accident and he was gone. We haven't seen him since."

In my world of overmedicated, undertraumatized intellectuals, I was viewed as an anomaly. I think I was even envied. I was someone who really had something, a real-life trauma, to pin all my troubles on. And I can name more than one artist's body of work that has been seriously influenced by my little tale of woe. I was a muse, a siren. "Hey you," I would whisper. "Come listen to this little ditty and go make a little something, something pretty, something profound, before you crash into my rugged shoreline."

"What are you taking?" my crying neighbor asked, awestruck, curious to know what drug was strong enough to blot out all the emotion that would be tied to having your father fry, bear the mark of a circus freak, and then leave you forever.

"Takin' care of business," I mouthed into my hospital coffee, like a stoner at a rock concert. I could have added in the air guitar if I wanted. Nobody here would give a shit. This was the loneliest place on earth.

13

JAMES PACKED the car completely different from my father.
He did everything completely different from my father. In fact,
James was just different, completely.

The morning we were set to leave for Cape Cod, he was
baking banana nut bread for the trip, sailing around the kitchen
like we weren't leaving for a week. He had a bandana on his
head, like a pirate, and was showing off his backyard, baby oil
prevacation tan, wearing cutoff shorts; a blue mesh tank top;
and flip-flops. He had a lot of muscles so it didn't look as bad
as you might imagine.

I walked by the bathroom and saw my mom curling her
eyelashes, to match her new, odd, layered haircut, compliments
of James.

"Are you ready, honey?" she said, appearing to pull her
head to look at me by dragging it by the eyelashes. "Don't
you have anything else to wear?" she asked, referring to my

longest, widest, and most worn-out pair of jeans. The bottoms were totally frayed from dragging on the ground for the entire school year. They were, in a word, perfect. I wore a black tank top, a beaded black choker necklace and matching bracelet. I also wore a serious amount of black eyeliner. Once your dad has been struck by lightning and wandered off in the middle of the night, you can get away with a lot of strange stuff, even if you are only ten. My mother shook her head very slowly so she wouldn't yank an eyelash out and looked defeated by my refusal to put on a different costume for this new sitcom of ours. She seemed to think she was Anne Romano from *One Day at a Time*. She had dyed her hair red and James had cut it into a sort of shag, all her hair coming forward toward her face. She was wearing a simple blue sundress, thank God. It was worse when she wore her hippy jeans around her too fat mother's butt. Actually the worst was when she and James danced while she was wearing her hippy jeans, my mother wiggling her butt, singing, "stayin' alive, stayin' alive!"

I schlepped my way past the bathroom and knocked on my sister's door. This house was smaller than our old one, but it somehow managed to squeeze in one extra bedroom, just enough space so that Anna and I could have separate rooms. Mine was the size of a large closet, hers the size of a small room, but bigger nonetheless. She always got more of everything. Not because she was the oldest but because she was the weirdest. It was just easier to give her what she wanted, so we did.

"Can I come in?" I asked, knocking hard enough to push the door open. The latches didn't stick unless you slammed the door really hard. She was sitting at her dressing table: a real live, showbiz-mirrored dresser with a little chair she could pull up to apply her makeup, do her hair, practice her lines. The chair had a puffy, floral pillow on it, with tiny ties to keep it attached to the wicker and wood. James seemed to know exactly what look Anna was going for and pulled the whole room together, one cheap piece at a time, from the local thrift store. He would walk into my room and throw up his hands in despair. There wasn't much even he could do with it. I was into all things psychedelic, except for the drugs, which I didn't do mainly because I didn't have any. He did buy me a black light poster with a peace sign on it and the black light to go along with it. He tossed them on my bed and said, "Girl, if you're gonna do this hippy chick thing, you might as well go for it all the way."

That had clearly been his motto for Anna's room, which was far more in keeping with his taste. Anna's interest in all things fancy had matured into an interest in all things shiny and glamorous. James had found pink, feathery boas to wrap around the bases of old lamps and sparkling, metallic fabrics to drape over an entire wall. When Aunt Sally came for Christmas, she took one look and said quietly to me, her hand making a sound barrier wall on one side of her mouth, "Well, let me guess who lives in this whorehouse." She turned to James and my mother, who were standing behind us in the hall holding hands like teenagers, and said, "This is great!"

Anna was wearing a dress, a summery number with large yellow and pink flowers cascading through a light green–striped background. She had her hair in some sort of old-fashioned hairdo, most of it tied back in a tight ponytail, the bangs clipped in a precise, straight line and plastered to her forehead. I didn't have the heart to tell her it wouldn't last, her smooth hair. Her curls would start to spring the minute she got outside. She was applying a pink, frosty lip gloss from a huge, fat tube. Her room smelled like lemons and roses, each scent fighting for the limited airspace. She turned to look at me while rubbing more lip gloss on her fat, lower lip, singing along with Peter Frampton.

"I'm in you," she sang with her mouth wide open, losing all the consonants but none of the emotion. She got up and turned off her eight-track player. This was a private thing between her and Peter Frampton, apparently. She sat back down and started to dump all of her makeup into a large straw bag with red straw flowers appliquéd on the side. We had very different notions about travel attire, I can tell you that. But then we seemed to have developed very different notions about everything.

I adjusted my backpack and went downstairs. James was singing "Do You Know the Way to San Jose?" while slicing his bread into perfectly sized travel pieces, placing two at a time into small plastic bags, then transferring the bags into a large plastic cooler. I looked into the cooler and could see the bottom was lined with canned sodas. On top of the sodas was a layer of Baggies holding sandwiches. One for James, my mother, Anna, and me. On top of that was another layer of Baggies, some filled with cookies, some with peanuts, some with carrots, and some with raisins. The banana nut bread was the final layer in James's travel cake.

"Hello, dark sister," he said dramatically. James said everything dramatically.

"He is so gay," my best friend Connie had remarked, early on, when he and my mother were first dating.

"I don't think so," I said, annoyed with her obvious stupidity. "They're getting married, you know," explaining the situation.

James was just, well, James. And as hard as I tried to dismiss him entirely, his enthusiasm was hard to ignore.

"Nice eyes," he commented. I looked up to see if he was being sarcastic. He was moving in for a closer look. "Very nice," he said, nodding his approval at my technique.

"Take that cooler out to the car," he requested. "Just stick it anywhere it fits," he said, laughing at an invisible joke. He had many invisible jokes.

I tried to lift the cooler but it was too heavy. James grabbed one side and helped me take it outside.

"You are going to L-U-V Provincetown," James promised. "And I have a little surprise for your sister, a side trip so she can honor one of her heroes. Or heroines, I should say." We shoved the cooler onto the seat and turned it sideways to serve as a barrier and armrest between my sister and me.

"Who?" I asked.

James mimed his answer, covering first his ears, then his

eyes, then his mouth. I thought he was doing "hear no evil, see no evil, speak no evil." I stood looking at him, dumbfounded.

He grabbed my hand and started rubbing his fist into my palm, fast and furiously, his fingers flying in and out, signing some gibberish to me.

"Helen Keller?" I asked suspiciously.

He threw his arms in the air in a gymnast's *V* for victory then held out his palm for a high five. I was not the sort of girl who went in for such physical displays of enthusiasm. In fact, enthusiasm was not really my thing. But James just had a way of coaxing us into acting like a TV family. I rolled my eyes and reluctantly slapped his hand with mine. He dropped his hand as though ending his winning Olympic floor routine. "Don't tell!" he warned.

My mother and Anna came out into the yard. Anna stood primly by the car, as though she were waiting for the chauffeur to come and take her to her next appointment. She stood there silently, with her oversized sunglasses, her old-fashioned straw bonnet, her schoolteacher's posture, while we did the work. Once you've spent an entire month indoors, afraid to leave the house, you aren't required to do much of anything.

14

"Mom, I'm going to go see Dad tomorrow," I said softly, trying to see if she could muster enough strength to talk to me.

I had pulled one of the straight-backed chairs up to the side of her bed and had moved as many of the accoutrements of the sick and the dying as I could. The rooms were so tiny that three used tissues and an empty juice box or two could render the space unnavigable. I tried to get in as close as I could to my mother, scooting the chair all the way up beside the metal side rails of her bed. I was as tired as I had ever been and the idea of standing beside the bed seemed akin to climbing Mount Kilimanjaro. It was no use. The chair was too low. I was talking to my mother's pillow.

I pushed the chair back and tried to stand up. I was totally exhausted. I felt like I had sandbags tied to my body and a few stuffed inside each organ. My brain was heavy too, like it was wrapped in a wet sleeping bag. I put my hands on my knees and stood up halfway, bending over like I had just completed a marathon and was waiting for my heart rate and breathing to begin to slow.

I completed the exercise and stood all the way up, dizzy. It occurred to me I ought to drink less coffee, quit smoking, eat right, and exercise. Then it occurred to me that I was about to go visit my father, whom I had not seen in twenty-four years and up to a few days ago I presumed to be dead, and further was about to ask my dying mother what she might know about this missing father/husband and the two decades of mis-information about his whereabouts. I decided to give myself a break on the health stuff.

"Mom, wake up," I said, leaning on the bed with my el-bows, facing her.

It looked like she was trying to wake up from a very un-pleasant dream. I had pulled her hair back into a pitiful little ponytail yesterday. My mother had wanted me to put her hair up. I didn't want to touch her at all, but she insisted. There wasn't enough for a twist or a bun even, and the bobby pins and hair clips I had brought from her condo hurt her head. I put some of my own hair gel on her slicked-back strands of hair to give them some weight and some texture. Every so often, her eyes would lose their flat, retarded glaze and regain their startling glimmer, the lapis lazuli blue that was the single thing that made my mother a real beauty, sometimes. She could register as handsome one second and leave no impres-sion the next. Then, whether it was a trick of the light or a twist of a mood, she could suddenly look absolutely stunning, the most beautiful creature you have ever seen. The other day, when she told me she knew where my father was, I had seen it for a split second, her willful magnificence. Then it was gone, hidden in her pain.

"Is Anna coming?" she asked, trying to rouse herself out of her own weary place.

"Uh, no, Mom, Anna isn't coming with me," I answered, assuming she wondered if Anna was going to go with me to see our father.

"No, is Anna coming here?" she clarified, working hard to make her words sound as she intended them to and to make herself known to me. She had almost completely lost the ability to sound like my mother, but she nailed it on that question.

"Mom, did you hear me? I'm going over to see Dad tomorrow," I repeated, hoping to divert her attention away from the Anna question. "What is he like?" I asked. That's what I really wanted to know. I really didn't care what he had done for two decades. Not yet. First, I wanted to know what he was going to look like and act like when I saw him. Was he going to be some diapered, blithering idiot with milk running down his chin? Or was he going to be a regular, older version of the dad I try to remember. The only picture I can maintain of my father before the lightning struck him is a series of images of him from behind. I can see him walking away. I can see his back, the back of his head. I can visualize him bent over fixing something I can't see, because his back is always to me.

"You must be tired, honey. Anna should come now," she

explained to me, closing her flat, not-so-beautiful eyes. She reached her hand out to find mine, landing on my forearm instead. She patted my arm gently, her hands ancient and freezing and soft, like some mummified angel. "You should just go home now."

After a few seconds of repose, she opened her eyes again and looked at me, startled, like I was not the daughter she was expecting. "Fun from rear?" she asked, her mother's voice back again, disgusted and dismayed. "What is that supposed to mean?"

She was referring to my baseball cap. I flipped it around and put it on the right way so could see the front.

"See. It says 'Run from Fear' this way," I explained, "and 'Fun from Rear' this way," I demonstrated, turning the cap around again, trying to keep it on my head so she couldn't see the dirty, hat-flattened hair it was hiding. "It's an artist's, umm, thing."

She looked at me as though I were explaining my alien abduction to her. I took the hat off.

"Mom," I pleaded, "can we talk about Dad for a minute?"

"He's fine," she said, sighing heavily, closing her eyes again. "You'll see. Is Anna okay?" she asked.

"Yes, she is, Mom," I replied.

"What is she doing? Why isn't she here?" my mother asked.

"She can't come, Mom. She just can't, okay?" I offered, looking for a pardon.

"Why?" she repeated firmly.

I looked away from her, turning my head toward the window. I saw the packages on the sill that had come from the museum. I had taken the two thick, manila envelopes out of the shipping box as soon as they arrived from Patrick three days ago. I hadn't been able to bring myself to open them up any further, to look at the photographs or to see what on earth this man, this burning hot photographer, was so eager for me to receive. I had carried them with me, unopened, back and forth from the hospital to the car to the condo. I reached over and picked up the thicker of the two packages. I knew it contained the prints of the work that Patrick wanted to show. I pulled the fat, paper tab that opened the padded envelope and removed a slim, cardboard box.

I opened the box and saw a stunning black-and-white photograph of a tree. It was taken in the dead of winter, from the looks of it. It was barren, gnarled, and totally impotent, standing alone in a frozen, muddy field against a bleak gray sky. I looked closer. I could see that there was life inside that ghastly looking tree, its blood dormant, beginning to pulse slightly, as it eagerly awaited the thaw. If trees had gender, this tree was male for sure. I held it up for my mother to see.

"Anna sent these," I began, "she wanted you to have them."

My mother didn't say a word. She just stared at me, curious.

"Oh . . . well . . . she did have a little trouble awhile back. Mainly she was worn out from taking care of the girls. You knew she went back to the, umm, spa, right?" I asked.

"She mentioned that," my mother said, warming up a bit.

After our unsettling family reunion at Anna's first detox, my mother refused to speak of it again. She stumbled into the topic one day on the phone when she was trying to remember when she had last seen her granddaughters. She paused then recalled she had spent a little time with them when they came to visit after Anna went to that "spa."

"Okay. Well, she started taking some pictures when she was there and it turns out she is really good at it. See?" I pulled out a few more photographs from the box, placing them on the ledge of the windowsill like it was a photo rail. "So now people are paying her to do this. She might even have a show soon."

"So why can't she come?" my mother asked tentatively.

"She's on assignment," I said, going for broke.

"Oh," my mother responded.

I knew that I had to do more, say more. It just didn't add up, even to my addled mother.

"She called me the other day. Remember when I told you I went to the pool at the condo? That day. She left a message saying she was coming as soon as she finished her assignment."

I held my breath as we both considered all the lies in the room, turning them over in our mouths, tasting them, deciding if we would swallow them up or spit them back out. We were far more used to the flavorless sin of omission.

My mother stared vacantly at the tree pictures for several minutes. "That's good," she said finally. She turned to look back at me. I watched as she blinked her eyes, finding me, bringing me back into focus. She stared at me intently, her eyes determined. She moved her hand, drawing it down my arm till it reached my hand.

"I think you could use a break," she said in a comforting tone that was only vaguely familiar. It was a voice she used for my sister, not me. She squeezed my fingers with surprising strength and closed her eyes.

15

My mother first met James at the library where he worked. His name was James Lleweinsky, which was just complicated enough of a name for us never, ever to use it. She went to the library once a week to get Anna her books during the month she wouldn't leave the house. I usually went with her to pick out my own books. It gave me a headache to watch my mother hanging over the desk flirting with James, but I kept going anyway. I tried very hard not to like him, but it seemed that every book he picked out for me was written just for me. He would sneak different kinds of books into my stack of girl detective novels, books like *The Outsiders*, *A Separate Peace*, *Lord of the Flies*, and *Diary of a Young Girl: Anne Frank*. I made the mistake of giving this book to Anna to read, who then narrowed the confines of her prison to the boundaries of her room, making the entire rest of the house off-limits, except for the bathroom.

Anna had a taste for epic romances. Since she didn't have anything else to do, she read *Gone With the Wind*, *Rebecca*, *Jane Eyre*, *Wuthering Heights*, and countless other big, fat, dreamy books that month. My mother made some sort of arrangement with the school because the teachers just shook their heads in sympathy and told me to tell Anna they couldn't wait to have her back at school. I thought it was great to be the only Greene girl in junior high school. Because even though she was a little nuts, she was a hard act to follow. She was such a brownnoser it was sickening. When asked, I told my friends that she was never coming back to school and that she would probably move to the East Coast to attend a private school for girls like her. I would point my finger toward my head and twist it around to indicate just what kind of girl I thought that was.

James had also picked Helen Keller's autobiography for me. I got the idea that Anna might see her self-imposed exile as a pretty stupid method of coping with a not-real handicap, so, hoping that Helen might inspire her to move boldly beyond the second-floor hallway, I tossed it on her bed for her to read. Instead, I would find Anna feeling her way around the perimeter of her room, a blind Anne Frank. Then she wouldn't talk for days at a time, and when she did she would make low, moaning noises. This was the deaf-mute phase of her solitary confinement. But when she wasn't feigning deaf, dumb, and blindness, she could talk about Helen Keller for hours. She seemed to know the whole book by heart and would quote passages as though she herself were a wise old woman who was actually brave enough to set foot out of the house, among other heroic acts.

"Few know what joy it is to feel the roses pressing softly into the hand," she would say, sitting on her bed cross-legged, rubbing her hands together with invisible lotion. She would take a deep breath and quiver, trying to hold back the tears from the sheer beauty of her stolen words. It was nauseating.

Anna's confinement, which had been brought on by a thunderstorm so violent our entire neighborhood had been without power for two days, came to an end one unremarkable evening. James, my mom, and I were sitting in the living room eating a pizza James had picked up on his way home from the library. We were sitting on the floor with our legs crossed, using the coffee table as our dining table. James made me use chopsticks to pick the mushrooms off my pizza and to bow tiny little bows with my hands pressed together when I wanted some more pizza or Coke to drink. It was his version of a Japanese dinner. We didn't know any Japanese words so we made them up.

We were saying "soy" and bowing to each other when Anna walked into the room. It took a moment for the importance of her entrance to register. It was the first time she had set foot on the first floor of the house in weeks. We froze in our prayerful positions, staring first at her then at each other. James said "ah so" and bowed deeply and respectfully in greeting. My mother and I followed his lead. Anna turned and ran out of the room and back up the stairs. We thought we had blown it. My mother said to leave her be.

I was dropping slimy mushrooms into the pizza box with my chopsticks when we heard her coming back down the stairs. We turned toward the doorway to look and watched her reenter the living room in her kimono robe and pink ballet slippers, her hair up in a high ponytail. She sat down at the end of the table, crossed her legs, and bowed to us. Anna was back, costume and all. We dealt with her return in the same way we dealt with her captivity, which was the same way we dealt with everything unusual or painful: we ignored it.

And even though she had been out of confinement for months, she still hadn't ventured past a handful of places, so our trip to Cape Cod was a huge deal that we all carefully ignored. We acted as though getting into the car and driving off to a faraway place for a vacation—the vacation a dreadful notion in and of itself from our experience—was an everyday occurrence. Anna would go to school, most of the time, and she would go to see James at the library or my mother at the tiny corner drugstore where she worked part-time. She hated to be in the car and walked to the few places she wasn't afraid of. The slightest sign of rain, including a certain type of wet-smelling wind or a fast-moving cloud, could send her straight back inside the house. If it were to actually begin to storm, she would run to her room, climb into her bed, and stay there, deep under the covers, until the storm passed. My mother would race home the minute she heard thunder or saw lightning and weather the storm with Anna, placing a pillow between Anna's head and the headboard to buffer the blows.

Anna liked to obliterate the sound of the storm by rocking back and forth on the bed, scrunched down in a little ball on her knees with the covers over her, knocking her head rhythmically into the headboard.

So it was practically a miracle that we were in a car at all with Anna. And it was surprising that she didn't have some sort of fit even sooner. We were hundreds of miles from home and fast approaching Massachusetts, according to the highlighted map that James had gotten from AAA, when it started. She had been silent for most of the trip, deeply engrossed in some trashy romance novel she bought for five cents outside a roadside supermarket where we had stopped to buy some peaches for James. He had a craving.

Anna's book had a woman with wild, jet-black hair looking up into the eyes of a very tall, very muscled man with long blond hair on the cover. He had on a white shirt with puffy sleeves and a frilly sort of collar. She was built like a Barbie doll, wearing a tight red dress that showed off her big boobs and her little waist.

Anna twirled her hair and read, hunched over the book in the backseat, across the cooler from me. I was looking at the map when I noticed she was twirling her hair faster and faster. I watched as she suddenly quit twirling it and pulled on it. From the look on her face, I guessed she was pulling it very hard. Her eyes were wide as though she was in pain and she was pressing her lips together, making funny little noises, like she was clearing her throat, over and over again. Her head moved slightly, back and forth, like she was banging it into an invisible headboard.

"Mom," I said, turning my eyes away from Anna for a second.

"What, honey?" she asked, turning around in her seat midlaugh, her left hand pulling away from the back of James's neck. She rubbed his neck constantly.

"James, stop the car," she commanded. He looked into the rearview mirror and saw Anna.

"Somebody needs a disco break!" he declared. He leaned toward the dash and pushed eject on the eight-track player. He pulled out a Patsy Cline tape and tossed it in the backseat like a happy-go-lucky litterer. It hit the cooler and startled us all, my mother, my sister, and me. Anna kept pulling her hair, but her throaty, clucking sounds became softer, almost imperceptible. She was still rocking back and forth but she kept her eyes glued to James's in the rearview mirror. He winked at her.

"Fay, can you hand me lucky tape number seven?" he requested. "I've gotta dance," he said, starting to make slow, alternating circles with his shoulders. "Thelma Houston, please!" he instructed in a frustrated stage whisper.

"Don't you think we might want to pull over?" my mother asked, turning to look at Anna while she popped the tape in. Anna kept rocking and clucking; her eyes locked into the rearview mirror, watching James watch the road until he could look back at her.

"Ladies, are you ready?" he asked, ignoring my mother's

question by taking her left hand in his right one and holding it high in the air.

"Lucy, grab your partner," he instructed. I looked out the window hoping he would find an alternate method of rescuing my sister if I ignored him.

"Lucy, I need your help," he implored. "We cannot dance alone," he said.

I looked over at my sister. I reached over to try to get her hand off her hair and into mine. She just yanked harder on her hair, pulling her whole head toward me.

The music was beginning to fill the car. "Never mind," James called out. "We don't need partners," he decided, letting go of my mother's hand but keeping his in the air, twirling it to the slowly accelerating beat.

"Don't leave me this way," he sang along, swaying his upper body back and forth, using his finger to keep the beat, pointing up, down, sideways, and back.

"Oh, baby," he crooned, taking both hands off the steering wheel to sweep them high in the air, bringing them together to point at Anna in the rearview mirror, "my heart is full of love and desire for you."

My mother grabbed the steering wheel while James continued his dance for Anna. My mother moved her shoulders awkwardly back and forth. Her only dance move was the retarded butt wiggle. I was completely antidisco but I danced my own hippy dance in the backseat for James's and my sister's benefit. I had shaken my hair in front of my eyes and was swinging it back and forth to the beat of the music. On one of my swings

I took a look over at Anna. Her lips were still pressed together, but I could see she was trying to hold back a smile as she danced her own private dance. She stared into the rearview mirror gazing gratefully at James, her finger twirling her hair to the beat of the music.

16

It was dusk when I pulled into the driveway to my mother's condominium. I stopped the car in the drive and began to remove the extraordinary amount of crap I had accumulated since I arrived in the Sunshine State. I used the fast-food bags for garbage bags, stuffing additional Styrofoam coffee cups, candy bar wrappers, and empty cigarette packs in them until they began to tear. I had four of these minitrash receptacles sitting beside the car. I crawled into the backseat to gather up all of the paper ephemera I had acquired.

I was a word hunter-gatherer. I would read every word on the back of a bottle of Comet cleanser then move on to the printed instructions about the insertion of a tampon and the dire warnings about toxic shock rather than sit on a toilet, bored, engaged in the usual bathroom activities. On my travels to and from the hospital I was an indiscriminate collector, picking up a Jehovah's Witness tract here, a right-wing political flyer there, and an assortment of hospital brochures on conjunctivitis, pregnancy, and carpal tunnel syndrome, to name a few. I had a pamphlet on planned giving opportunities at the hospital and a leaflet on new recycling rules for the complex. If it was made of paper and had words on it, I would pick it up and read it. Then I would toss it in the backseat.

I had my arms filled with paper and was backing out of the car when I stepped on one of the small to-go bags, knocking it to the ground, its contents scattering. I tried to avoid stepping on any of the other bags and rose up too quickly, hitting my head on the edge of the roof of the car and dropping the wadded-up trash I was holding. I banged my skull so hard I dropped to a kneeling position, pressing on the back of my head to help make the pain go away. I thought I would either faint or throw up.

"Oh, fuck me," I swore, coming to my senses, having known all along I should have gotten a stupid, fucking garbage bag out of the garage first. I got up slowly, ignoring the mess of paper that was beginning to skulk around the driveway in the muggy, evening breeze. I leaned back into the car, grabbing the atlas and the package from Kyle and shoving them under one arm. I tried to organize the overdue library books and the books I had brought with me, herding them with my free arm into a couple of neat stacks, rounding up *The Tibetan Book of Living and Dying* and *On Death and Dying* with my oversized photography books from the floor. I had a fleeting notion to return the library books in the morning before heading east then dismissed the thought entirely. Somehow, the idea of returning things on time and thus not having to pay outrageous fees for them was about as attractive to me as quitting smoking and exercising regularly.

"Ooh." I heard a loud sigh behind me. I carefully extricated myself from the car, bending low to avoid hitting my head again. It was Bella, crouched down, picking up bits of paper and trash and stuffing them into a white plastic garbage bag. Feeling instant pangs of both guilt and shame, I scrambled for the rest of the garbage, running back and forth down the drive, grabbing for a flyer about the grand opening of a miniature golf course in which the breeze had taken a particular interest. I helped Bella get back up to her feet and took the plastic bag from her, stuffing the remaining garbage I had collected deep into the bag.

"Thanks," I managed. "I'm going over to the gulf coast tomorrow. It got so windy," I offered, a weak explanation for how a carful of garbage got dumped out onto a dying woman's driveway in the Mandarin Mist community of Boca Siesta, Florida.

"So you're going to see your father," she said, putting her hands on her ample hips, her head dropping to one side.

I couldn't believe it. This goddamn stranger knew more about my father than I did. I didn't know what to say. I was speechless.

"Well, my dear, it's about time," she said, breaking the silence.

Bella put her hand on my shoulder and gave it a little

STACY

SIMS

squeeze. I couldn't tell whether she was reprimanding me or consoling me. I stiffened and held my breath.

I looked down and remembered the atlas.

"Can you tell me the best way to go?" I asked, hoping that if I listened to literal directions for a minute or two I might be able to clear my head and think of a question for Bella that might help me to navigate the grander scheme.

"Oh, honey, I don't drive," she laughed. "Your mother used to take me to dialysis in this big old car of hers. That's when she told me about your father, James, Red Dog, you, your sister. She could tell a story, your mother. You all had quite a life, didn't you?"

Did we? Well, okay, of course we did. But what in the fuck had my mother told her? We just didn't talk about it, any of it, ever. My mother never mentioned my father, and after Sweet Home, none of us spoke of James. I had never even met her third husband, Red Dog, so I couldn't care less about him. I had no idea what this woman believed she knew about my life. I decided this must be what amnesia feels like, when someone is speaking to you as though you surely know what they are talking about, all the details behind the words, all the memories associated with the names. My heart was racing but my mind was blank. I couldn't latch on to a single, coherent thought. I closed my eyes and rubbed my temples. I could taste metal in my mouth.

"You'll be fine, Lucy," Bella comforted. "Your mother says she always knew you would be okay. She says that you were born strong. Your sister, now there's another story, eh? Your mother thinks she needs to grow up."

I wanted to scream. Why in the world was my mother telling all of our stuff, our whole mess of a family story to some fat, old, foreign lady who lives across the street, peppering it with commentary reflecting her own newfound wisdom and clarity?

"Oh, yeah, right," I scoffed. Bella looked hurt. "I'm sorry. I have got to go inside and get some rest," I said. "I'm exhausted," I offered, a half-assed apology for making this woman somehow responsible for my family's mess.

"Earl over there can help you with the directions," she said, unperturbed, waving to the Orchid Man. "He used to work for the state. Education or something. He traveled all over Florida until his skin got so bad." According to Bella, he had skin that literally fell off if he bumped it. It crumbled like parchment paper, like an old manuscript that shouldn't be handled under any circumstances. He wore gloves most of the time, his arms crossed at the wrists, his hands lying in his shrunken, old man's lap. He sat watching over his orchids in a folding chair someone had set up on his front porch. His rheumy eyes spilled over constantly, so he looked to be crying all the time. And now he slowly lifted his gloved hand and waved. It was the salutelike gesture of a military man. These fucking neighbors were dead set on being helpful.

"I'm sorry," I said to Bella, turning to go into the house with my map and my package. "I . . . I'm sorry."

"I'll get someone to drive me to see your mother tomorrow," Bella said, turning to walk back across the street to her own condo. "Don't you worry about a thing. You'll be fine. You're a good daughter," she assured me.

"I'll take my mom's car. Here, take these," I said, tossing her the keys to the rental. She looked at me quizzically and reminded me in a whisper, "Honey, I don't drive."

"I know!" I responded. I was getting madder by the second. I was trying so hard not to be an asshole but it seemed out of my control. All of it. "Have Mrs. Albright drive this car. It's nicer."

I had to get inside. It was so fucking hot. I said "Sorry" again and opened the door to my mother's condo. I walked straight to the refrigerator and yanked out a beer from the six-pack I bought a few days ago. I slammed the map and the package on the counter and twisted off the bottle cap. I pinched the curvy edge of the cap between my index finger and my thumb and snapped it against the sliding glass patio door. It didn't make enough noise so I went and retrieved it. I stood back a bit farther, arching my elbow in the air, and snapped the bottle cap again. It hit the glass hard and sounded like it. I took a big swig of beer to celebrate. Then I took another. I had a brief thought of doing something good for me, like taking a walk or going to a movie. I chugged the rest of the beer, quickly washing away any notion of taking better care of myself.

I looked at the package from Kyle. I picked it up and turned it over to examine the back side of the large manila envelope. I threw it back down on the counter, sending it flying over the edge and down to the floor, along with a bunch of mail I'd been ignoring on behalf of my mother. I got another beer from the refrigerator along with a piece of cold, stiff pizza. I sat on the floor in a tiny pool of light from the day's fast-fading sun, putting my beer on the floor beside me. I picked one of the smaller envelopes up off the floor with my free hand. I took a bite of pizza while examining the letter. It appeared to be a solicitation for a low-interest credit card. I dropped it and picked up another one. I presumed it was a copy of an invoice for her condo fees, as a similar-looking envelope came for me monthly. George and Anna paid the mortgage, I paid the fees. That was our deal.

I picked up the big envelope again and examined it. Kyle had printed my whole name, Lucille Myrna Greene. He had spelled out "care of" rather than writing "c/o." He had written out his name and address in the upper left-hand corner. Kyle Stephen McDaniels, 2746 Professor Street, Tremont, Ohio. No zip code. I reached my hand high and put the pizza crust back up on the counter beside me. I took another sip of beer and set the bottle back down.

The light was beginning to disappear. I ripped the envelope open and pulled out its contents. I peeled away a thin layer of white tissue paper and pulled apart two pieces of cardboard to reveal a single eight-by-ten black-and-white photograph and a small piece of parchment paper. I held up the photograph to view it in the remaining sliver of sunlight. It was a picture of a young girl leaning up against the trunk of a craggy, old tree with her back to the camera. Her blond hair was pulled back in a ponytail held by a long, dark ribbon. She wore a dress with a tiny floral print and was barefoot, her feet small and white against the base of the humongous, exposed roots of the tree. She was leaning with her head down and her arms high, her fingers splayed out against the tree. She looked like she was trying with all her might to hold the tree up. Either that, or she was resting against it, utterly exhausted. I picked up the small piece of paper.

"You can be healed without being cured" was all it said.

The last light of the day faded away. I sat on the floor looking at the photograph in the dark and I stayed there well into the night.

17

WE DROVE ALONG without further incident toward our first vacation since my father got struck by lightning. Having recovered from her moment of terror over God knows what, Anna continued to read her steamy novel; I read little paragraphs about historic points of interest in the Trip-Tik map book. My mother and James played with each other's hands and talked nonstop. They chattered constantly, so much so that I couldn't hear a single thing they were saying as the conversation tumbled into the backseat. It sounded like, "Word, word, wordy word, word, ha ha ha! Wordy word word." I would take an occasional interest, mainly when I heard "word, word, word, Lucy, word."

"What?" I would say. "What about me?"

They would laugh and my mother would say, "Nothing, dear." It was so gross. It wasn't that I wanted her to be unhappy, exactly. It was just that she had been unhappy for as long as I had known her, until James. And it just seemed *so* fake, her laugh, her hair, everything, especially their lovey-dovey, touchy-feely crap. I knew something wasn't right, but it was a far better version of wrong than I had ever known. And I wasn't about to point out that our life was still all screwed up because I didn't want to lose James.

So I just kept quiet. I went back to my map and read more about the Boston Massacre and the graveyard where Paul Revere and John Hancock are buried. I saw a map to Paul Revere's house and the site of the Battle of Bunker Hill. All of this was slightly interesting because we had learned about it in school. But mainly I read because I liked to look at words on a page. It didn't matter much to me what they were.

"Look up Plymouth Rock in there, Luce," James called back. I flipped back a couple of pages and found it on the map.

"Okay," I said, indicating I had completed my mission.

"What does it say?" James asked.

"The stone is said to have been three times as large, in 1620 when the *Mayflower* docked, as it is today," I read as quickly as I could, in a bored monotone. "It was moved from the original location, broken in two, and after many years returned to the original site. It has been put back together with masonry." I loved to read but I hated to read aloud.

"Sounds great, let's go." James thought everything sounded great. He was up for anything.

We pulled into the park less than half an hour later and got out of the car. It was the first time I had ever smelled sea air, salty air. It smelled great. Anna emerged from her side of the car. She had her sunglasses on and was arranging her large, straw hat on her head, tying two long ribbons in a bow under her chin. She had read way too many accounts of southern belles in distress. She took a whiff of the coastal air and pinched her nose closed, making a face.

"Let's go see this rock!" James chimed, snapping his fingers back and forth, keeping time to each syllable.

We hiked toward an impressive open monument where hundreds of people were gathered. James led the way, making us hold hands so we could snake through the other vacationing families like a human chain. He guided us straight toward a break in the wall of tourists and positioned us, shoulder to shoulder, for our first viewing of a historic relic. We peered down into the open pit and looked upon a big, boring rock, surrounded by a bunch of litter. You could see the remains of graffiti on the wall of the base of the pit, where some park official had unsuccessfully tried to erase "this rock sucks."

"Hmm," my mother commented.

Anna continued to pinch her nose. It was unclear if the face she was making was in response to the smell of the air or the sight of the rock.

I looked up at James. Before my dad got struck by lightning, Anna and my mother dictated the family mood. When Anna wasn't afraid or my mother wasn't mad, we were happy. After the lightning, it was Anna's show entirely. When she wasn't freaked out we were relieved, me and my mom. But now we let James decide how we ought to respond to things.

He had his arms folded over his chest, his brow creased, as though he was pondering something of extreme importance.

"This rock does suck," he concluded loudly, causing a chorus of gasps from the other families around us. "Let's go, girls. We have bigger fish to fry."

He grabbed my mother's hand, she grabbed mine, and I grabbed Anna's, and we snaked back through the tourists who were making their own pilgrimage toward the rock.

"The rock sucks," Anna whispered. James stopped dead in his tracks. We ran into him and each other like dominoes and turned to stare at Anna.

My mother began in a scolding tone, "That's not—"

"That's right, Anna. That rock does suck. And it is our job to inform the masses!" James interrupted. My mother looked confused. In one glance, James let her know exactly what he was up to. At least as I read it, his raised eyebrows seemed to scream to my dense mother, "For God's sake, Fay, let me handle this!" She turned to me and shrugged, as though to say, "I give up."

"Come with me, Anna," James summoned. He took her hand and they set off down the hill together. My mother and I followed them. We could hear him whispering to the ascending families, "Psst. Hey you, yeah you. The rock sucks." Anna chimed in every once in a while, mainly on the word *sucks*.

My mother put her arm around me. I jumped, startled. We didn't touch each other. She looked pissed, as though this were my fault, the fact that we didn't have a close relationship. She took a deep breath. "James thinks Anna has a lot of pent-up feelings," she shared. "He wants us to try to draw her out," she coached, a wise and observant mother helping her younger daughter navigate life's difficulties.

"Duh!" I responded. It was amazing how stupid my mother could be. Or maybe it was amazing how stupid she thought I was. She was the one who had never, ever, once mentioned my father since he left. Not once.

"So we'll talk about Dad and the lightning and all that, right?" I asked, knowing the answer in advance.

"Well, no. James disagrees with me on this, but he will respect my wishes. I just don't think it does anyone any good to dwell on that, particularly Anna," she preached.

"Well, that sucks," I said.

My mother, with her arm still around me, tightened her grip on my arm and squeezed it really hard. I tried to pull away from her but she wouldn't let me. "You stop it, Lucy. Just stop it. I am doing the best I can and you just have to stop fighting me," she demanded, her voice low, her teeth clenched. Then she did the worst thing of all. She started to cry. She put her free hand over her face so no one could see. She still had a tight grip on me but now she held me like she needed me, as though I was supposed to comfort her. I stared straight ahead and didn't say a word. When we reached the bottom of the hill, she let me go. I ran as fast as I could to catch up with James and Anna.

As we pulled back onto the expressway toward Boston, my

mother wriggled her hand between the seat and the door, waving it in the space behind the seat. I moved my knees toward my sister, and watched her hand searching for me unsuccessfully. She pulled her arm back through to the front seat, defeated, unable to reach me with her stupid stick of gum.

18

I was halfway across the state of Florida by 11:00 a.m., drinking my third diet Coke and eating Cheez Doodles in an attempt to ease the pain of my beer hangover. I had gone to bed late, after 2:00 a.m., and slept restlessly. I woke up five hours later when the phone rang. I had tried to think what a good daughter might wear to see her father, a father who hasn't laid eyes on her since she was six and who may or may not give a shit about seeing her, regardless of what she might be wearing. I ignored the phone, as it rang again and again, and found a semi-tasteful tank-style black cotton sundress in my mother's closet. I paired it with sandals, the least offensive pair of shoes my mother owned. I pulled my hair back into a ponytail and put my ball cap on, then took it off. I had the idea that a baseball cap might be confusing for my father. Then I had the idea that *I* might be confusing for my father. I left the hat off anyway.

I was listening to the car radio, alternating between static-filled country-western and equally static-filled Cuban stations. The only stations that seemed to have divine broadcast power were the evangelical stations. I heard a harrowing tale of a man's struggle with alcohol, drugs, guns, the law, and women, and his awesome redemption through Our Christ, The Lord. I was thinking about being saved myself when the air-conditioning started to whine. I flipped the switch to low. It whined more slowly. I pushed it up to high again. It whined to a stop. I moved the switch back and forth. The air conditioner in my mother's car was dead.

"Christ," I swore.

"Summertime and the sinnin' is easy!" the radio chastised.

"Shut up," I responded, turning off the radio. I was now driving through the flat, dry middle of Florida with the sun beating down on my mother's huge, black sedan in hot, sticky silence, fully aware that the rental car with the functional air conditioner was most certainly sitting unused in my mother's driveway.

"Fuck! Fuck! Fuck!" I screamed, beating on the steering wheel. I hated this state. I hated it passionately. I looked around at the landscape with a loathing eye. I hated the flat, parched terrain; it had no beauty in it, not even a desolate beauty. It was a goddamn swamp outlined by a beach, a stalker chick with alluring eyeliner. I stared straight ahead. I refused to get involved with the scenery.

I wiped the cheesy film off my right hand onto the hot seat of the car. I was stuck with myself for another hour, at least, with nothing to look at and nothing to listen to. I was forced to drive on with only my thoughts, the stillness molding them, the sun baking them. I wished I had bought some aspirin at the mini-mart. I had taken the last two I could find at my mother's house when I hung up the phone after talking with my sister's caseworker.

"Lucy?" she had asked as I answered the phone at the fucking crack of dawn.

"Yeah," I replied, trying to wake up.

"This is Lauren Feigen from Meadowhurst," she said quickly and firmly, as though she had just explained everything I needed to know about her. There is a certain tone those without any real authority use to imply that they have some. I knew the trick. I used it when I called from the museum.

"Okay," I mustered.

"How are you this morning?" she asked in a cheerful yet concerned tone.

"Okay," I repeated.

"Well, Lucy, I'm calling to report on your sister's progress here at Meadowhurst," she offered. "Do you have a minute?"

"I guess," I replied. I was not in the mood to grant this person one quarter of an inch of goodwill. I had met her before. At Anna's first rehab, at Sweet Home, her counselor's name was Melissa Banks. At Meadowhurst, the last time Anna was there, I had to deal with Lil "short for Lillian" Gephardt. I knew enough about psychology to understand that my strong, negative reactions to these recovery experts might just reveal something about my own issues. But having already attended two intensive family therapy sessions with my sister and a Melissa/Lil/Lauren facilitator, I can tell you that these people are determined to take the entire family down on a very deep dive, regardless of whether anyone is capable of doing so. My mother attended the first one at Sweet Home in Texas. I don't think she ever quite recovered from it. Not surprisingly, the entire episode was never mentioned again. We were not the kind of people to go looking for buried treasure. We were the ones who hid it in the first place.

But it is these people's job to bring suppressed family issues to the surface. And they aim to do so quickly so their charges feel as though they have uncovered at least a tiny piece of buried treasure. They want to hand off a gold bullion for their sober patient to work with once their month is up and they need to carry forth in the real world, sea legs and all. They are not concerned, seemingly, that they have given everyone else involved a serious case of the bends and no clear direction back to shore. To be fair, it is possible that some sort of debriefing and navigational assistance gets covered on the last day. I never bothered to conclude either of the Family Weekend sessions.

"Lucy, Anna is doing much better now. Her detox was pretty intense because of her dual addiction, well, actually her triple addiction, although we don't do too much with food issues right away. Or her shopping issues for that matter. And the doctors haven't ruled out depression either. But just getting her off the alcohol and the antianxiety drugs has been enough of a challenge. She is as paralyzed by the agoraphobia as she is by the alcoholism. I'm telling you more than I should, but I think this is probably familiar to you by now, Lucy." They all had the same trick, using my first name repeatedly as though this was all really about me and not my sister.

"Mm, hmm," I mumbled in agreement. Yes, this was familiar to me.

"I have been told you are spending some time with your mother and that she is not well," Lauren stated. "Is that so?" she asked, to clarify. Addicts are notorious liars. I'm sure Lauren has been laughed at and hung up on by family members who have heard one wild story too many from a parent, a child, or a sibling.

"Yes, this is so," I replied, enjoying the cadence of this courtroomlike repartee.

"Lucy, it would be really important to Anna's recovery if you could come here next weekend to participate in our Family Weekend." These people were very direct. I did appreciate that. It made it easier for me to cut to the chase.

"Well . . . ," I began, then yawned, sitting up in bed and looking at the alarm clock. It read 7:02 A.M. Something occurred to me. She was calling from Arizona.

"What time is it there?" I asked her.

"Five A.M.," she replied. "I wanted to make sure I spoke to you. Anna says she has left messages for you and you haven't returned her calls."

"She left one message for me, Lauren," I replied, emphasizing her name to clarify my authority and to remind her that I wasn't the sister back in rehab for the third fucking time. "She left one message."

"But Lauren," I continued, "could you ask her about some messages she got from a friend of my mother's, oh, a couple of months ago? Can you ask her about that? Can you ask her about the conversation she had where she was told that my mother was very sick? Can you ask her why she forgot to do anything or tell anyone about that? Lauren, can you do that for me?" I was wide-awake now. I was seriously hungover but my mind was crystal clear.

"Because I feel," I said, drawing out the word *feel* to show her I know the recovery drill. "I feel," I repeated, "that it would be very helpful for me to know the answer to that question the next time someone at the hospital asks me why it took so long for my mother to see a doctor. Usually they ask this when they're adjusting her morphine drip to relieve her excruciating pain. It makes me feel, yes feel, bad that by the time I found out and came down here, it was too late for them to do anything but fill her up with drugs so she can die in peace, or at least without so much pain. Because Anna told Bella she was coming down and she never did. She never told me, she never called my mother, and she never did anything. So can you ask Anna about that, Lauren?" I shouted.

"Lucy, I know you're feeling very angry," she observed. "That's why it would be important for you to come out here for the weekend, to help Anna understand the consequences of her using."

"How about this? You tell Anna I'm coming there. And tell

her I'm bringing Mom too," I proposed, with enthusiastic sarcasm dripping all over my words. "That way, both Anna and my mother will be expecting a visit from the person they most want to see but aren't ever going to see again. Know why, Lauren?" I asked. "Because my mother is dying and she is dying fast. She might even die today while I am visiting my father."

Lauren gasped, audibly. She had read the family history.

"Yep, him. Mr. Sizzle and Split. That's a whole different story for another time. But since my mother is dying, she'll just have to imagine she saw Anna and Anna will just have to make believe she saw her mother. Maybe Anna can make believe she remembered to call me to tell me Mom was sick while she's at it."

"Anna is working on getting to the truth of things, Lucy," Lauren said, reprimanding me slightly. "That's why it would be really helpful to have you here. To offer your view of things. And maybe to set the record straight about your feelings." She was trying to lure me in. "She says you've been a really good sister."

I looked at the clock. It was 7:17 A.M. I hung up the phone. I couldn't think of a single thing to say.

The phone continued to ring while I was getting dressed to go. I caught it between rings and called the hospital to check on my mother. I was told she was sleeping. I could hear it ringing again as I walked down the driveway to the car. I waved to Earl, the Orchid Man. He was an early riser. He saluted me with a gloved hand, sending me off to see my father, alone.

19

JAMES CLAIMED HE had an errand to run in Boston before we went out to our rental cottage on the Cape. He said he needed to pick up a package for a friend back in Cleveland, that it was something too fragile to mail.

"What is it?" Anna asked.

"It's a glass bird," James lied. "It's a tiny hummingbird made of glass. It is very fragile, as you might imagine."

"Who is it for?" Anna asked, taking an uncharacteristic interest in the details of James's charade. I was feeling an uncharacteristic moment of panic myself with the thought that these two might become close. She had been so remote for so long, I pretty much had had James to myself. Except for when he was with my mother.

"It's for Ginger at the library," James responded, remarkably at ease with his made-up story. I began to think we might actually pick up a small package, either before or after we arrived at the Helen Keller school.

"Why do we have to pick up a stupid glass bird for Ginger?" my mother asked. She was still upset with me. I ignored her anger and focused on the fact that I was the only one in on James's secret plan. Ha!

"She told me that she knows of a special store in Boston," I offered. Both my mother and Anna turned to look at me. They both peered suspiciously, my mother over her sunglasses and Anna from under her retarded bonnet.

"What?" I asked with my hands in the air, palms up, to indicate my innocence.

"Lucy helped me lock up the other night. Ginger just couldn't stop talking about her bird. Whenever she talks about her 'menagerie' she is transformed into a southern girl, hoopskirts and all. Too much Tennessee Williams on slow days, I guess," James speculated.

"It's in Watertown," James continued. "Lucy, look that up on that map of yours," he requested, winking at me. That seemed to do the trick for my mother and Anna. They turned to look out of their respective windows. They were quiet. Maybe they were also contemplating this image of Ginger, her heavy bottom stuffed into a hoopskirt, moving through a dark and cluttered apartment, trying not to knock tiny glass figurines off the coffee table, the bookcase, the curio cabinet.

"Here we are," he announced while I was still trying to find Watertown on the map. We pulled into a narrow driveway, through an open pair of iron gates. Neither Anna nor my mother seemed to notice the sign posted at the gate. It would have been a dead giveaway. We pulled into a small parking lot surrounded by manicured lawns, winding sidewalks, and giant, ancient trees and got out of the car. We stood in front of a very large redbrick building with an impressive four-pointed tower. It was surely the oldest building I had ever seen.

"Is this the store?" Anna asked warily.

Just then, a woman and a young boy came out of the building and headed down the sidewalk toward us. She walked slowly, taking a step every five seconds or so. The boy, who looked to be about our age, was holding on to her arm. He was wearing extremely dark sunglasses and was tapping on the sidewalk in front of him with a long stick, making little half circles in front of them as they shuffled toward us.

"Surprise!" James announced.

Anna stood perfectly still, staring openmouthed at the boy, her bonnet tipped to one side, her own sunglasses perched on the edge of her nose. I have to admit, I was a little startled myself. There was nothing pretty about this blind boy. And as they came closer to us, you could hear him making sounds. He was craning his neck, looking up toward the sky then back down toward the sidewalk, making odd shapes with his mouth and barking like a seal. He was creepy.

"I'm confused," my mother admitted. I laughed nervously. She gave me a dirty look.

"James, where are we?" she asked in the stern voice of our real mother, overriding the happy-go-lucky accent of our fake mom, the one who tried to trick James and Anna.

"We are at the Perkins School for the Blind!" James announced gleefully.

We all stared at him.

"Where Helen Keller went to school! This is the place!" he enthused. My mother and Anna stared at the barking blind boy then looked back at James, horrified. "It's a little side trip for Anna," he confessed, beginning to sound almost apologetic.

"What a nice idea, James," my mother allowed, through clenched teeth.

"Let's go inside," James coached. Anna was still firmly rooted at the base of the sidewalk, about to be a major obstacle for the blind boy and his seeing-eye woman. His stick was tap, tap, tapping closer and closer to Anna's perfectly white Keds.

"Can he see me at all?" Anna asked the boy's companion. The woman smiled kindly and shook her head no.

"Can he hear me?" Anna asked. The woman shook her head again. I thought perhaps she was mute.

"Anna, get out of the way," my mother scolded. And she did. Only she waited until the exact moment when the boy's cane would have tapped her shoe instead of the sidewalk to hop aside. She stood close as he passed, leaning toward him, to see if he might somehow detect her presence. The boy tapped and barked his way right past her.

James was all the way up to the door of the main building. My mother was close behind him, struggling to let her new mother persona, the enthusiastic, up-for-anything one come out to play. She lifted her chin a bit and her second personality emerged, defiant. She motioned for us to follow with a big jaunty scoop of her arm and a nod of her head toward the massive, wooden double doors.

Anna adjusted her glasses, retied the bow on her hat, and without looking at me, walked quickly past me toward James and our mother. I ran to catch up, making loud wooden clunking noises with my clogs. Anna turned to stare at me, looking down at my feet in a silent big-sister reprimand.

"They can't hear us either. Most of them are deaf too," I informed her with my Trip-Tik knowledge, stomping even louder. "You should try reading about something besides sex," I continued. "You just might learn something." I clomped my way right into the darkness of the main building.

"Shhh!!" my mother and James shushed me in unison.

Both Anna and I took off our sunglasses and blinked, adjusting our eyes to the darkness. There were bricks everywhere, on the walls, the floor, and the ceiling. It looked like the dungeon of a very nice castle. The ceilings were low and all the red bricks made for a cavelike excursion into the center of the building. There were small, yellow lights illuminating the hallway. It was very, very quiet. I tried to tiptoe on my clogs, but the wooden heels kept falling to the floor.

"Shhh!!" Anna said, joining my mother and James.

We didn't see any people, not blind ones or deaf ones or regular ones. We snuck through Helen Keller's school like bandits.

We came upon a large, cavernous space in the center of the building. The ceiling was at least twice as high as the hallway, and the room was equally wide. There were large wooden cases on each side of the room and between each case were large library tables. The room seemed bright in comparison to the halls. The cases were filled with all kinds of weird things, like stuffed birds and raccoons, wooden blocks, kitchen utensils, books, and a giant, empty snake skin. Everything was covered in dust. I thought it was a good thing the kids at this school were blind. Otherwise, this stuff would scare them to death.

"Haahh!" James exclaimed in a whisper, pointing up. At the end of the room, up above a railing, was a giant black-and-white picture of Annie Sullivan and Helen Keller. He dropped to his knees and bowed down. When he straightened back up, he beckoned for Anna. She walked over and stood next to him, refusing to look down where he was kneeling. Instead, she looked over her right shoulder, as though fascinated with the side of one of the cases.

"Anna, meet Annie and Helen. Annie and Helen, this is Anna Greene, one of your biggest fans," James said politely to the mural and to the back of Anna's head. Suddenly, this plan was beginning to bug me. I was starting to get really sick of all this James and Anna business.

I clunked my way to the side of the room, calling attention to the fact that I was leaving the area. They all ignored me, James and Anna knelt in fake prayer and my mother bent over one of the cases for a closer look at some dead rodent. So I kept going. There were a series of tiles spaced out along the wall, each with a different raised picture on it. I guessed it was for the blind kids, these Braille illustrations. There was a lion and a book and a piano. I closed my eyes and began to blindly feel my way out of the room. I shuffled my feet so I wouldn't make so much noise, now working on a silent escape. They wouldn't even know I was gone until it was too late! When I reached the void of a doorway or a window, I would open my eyes a little bit, then close them back tight after finding my next guiding wall. It wasn't easy being a blind girl on the lam.

The sounds of my family—Anna now a chatty girl genius, spewing one Helen Keller quote after another, James and my mother cheering her on—started to fade as different sounds became clear to my blind girl's sharp ears. I could make out a piano and some clapping and some stomping. I heard words too, but they were muffled. I felt my way along the walls toward the music, trying to figure out the pictures on the tiles along the way. To me, it all felt the same; bunched-up tile against smooth tile. I would be a terrible blind girl. I cheated and opened my eyes into narrow slits, trying to convince myself that my fingertips had known I was touching a chair, a bird, a snake.

Suddenly, the wall I was feeling up gave way to an open void so I opened my eyes again just a crack to see where I was. I was standing by a doorway, having discovered the source of the noise. It was coming from a tiny, little church: a chapel, the sign said. It was a regular sign for seeing people. I pressed myself close to the wall just outside and peeked around the doorway for a better look. I withdrew my head quickly to think all this through, ditching the blind charade in favor of Lucy, girl detective. There must have been forty kids in there, from very small children to teenagers. A couple of them looked almost like regular kids, but most of them looked like the boy outside. More like crippled, retarded kids than plain old blind ones. I peeked back in and realized no one could see me so I stepped into the doorway and watched.

There was a woman playing the piano. She appeared to be blind too. Her eyes were milky white and she looked up into the corner of the room where there was nothing to look at while she played. She was playing a song I remembered from my brief Sunday school experience. The children were either singing, loudly and horribly out of tune, or keeping the beat, badly, with their feet or their hands. But the lady at the piano sang sweet and clear, cutting through all of the enthusiastic, terrible noise of her congregation.

Amazing grace! How sweet the sound,
That sav'd a wretch like me!
I once was lost, but now am found,
Was blind, but now I see.

This was the most confusing thing I had ever heard: blind kids in church singing about how they was blind but now they see. I clapped my hand over my mouth to try to keep from laughing. It wasn't funny, exactly, but that's what my body wanted to do. It was either that or cry, and the fact that I felt like crying was even more confusing than the blind kids singing about seeing. I was pretty sure this all had to do with God somehow. I knew we should have gone to church for more than one summer of Sundays. I backed away from the chapel and began down the long, dark hallway. I clomped hard and made as much noise as I could. I wanted to stomp out the noise of the choir. I wanted to override the confusion in my head. I wanted to get the hell out of Helen Keller's school and get back to the familiar discomfort of my heathen family.

I discovered them outside, way down the sidewalk near a huge playground. I could see my mother had found a bench. Having made it through something that might be considered educational, she was rewarding herself with a cigarette. James and Anna were huddled around a drinking fountain. At first I thought they were messing around trying to get a drink, pushing each other out of the way. As I came closer I realized what they were doing and was deeply thankful that there were no other witnesses, blind or otherwise.

James was pumping wildly on the foot pedal of the drinking fountain, scooping up water with his right hand and dumping it into Anna's outstretched palm. She had her eyes closed and her mouth open like she was retarded. James was scooping water then pressing his fist into Anna's wet hand, spelling out something in his crazed version of sign language. Suddenly, a look of absolute joy washed over Anna's face and she began to mouth her own bad version of the word James had been signing into her palm.

"Wahdah, wahdah," she moaned, in her retarded-sounding deaf, dumb, and blind person's voice.

"Hallelujah!" James cried out. "She has been saved. She can speak!" he celebrated.

Anna began to jump up and down, clapping her hands, her eyes open and her face filled with light. It was unclear whether she was celebrating Helen's breakthrough or her own but she looked for a minute like Anna of long ago, Anna before my father got struck by lightning, Anna in the middle of some fantastic, dramatic performance. Her bonnet had fallen to the ground and her hair was beginning to spring free from the strange shape she had forced upon it. James waved me over, indicating he wanted me to join their celebratory jig. I did it just so I could clomp on Anna's bonnet. And after a few rings around the water fountain, I lost my focus on ruining Anna's hat and noticed that this was really sort of fun. My mother remained on the bench despite James's efforts to get her to join us. She sat there and watched us, flicking her cigarette, smiling. For a single, magical second it felt real, like we actually were a happy family. I turned to smile back at my mother. She wasn't looking. She had turned her head and was staring into the distance, distracted by something we couldn't see.

STACY

SIMS

20

I followed the directions that Aunt Martha had given me. The highway gave way to their dense neighborhood without much warning. The houses were small and it looked more like a trailer park than a housing development. If these same houses, in the same condition, were picked up and dropped into a northern city, it would surely be considered the bad part of town. Here the dense, green jungle grass, the palm trees, and a scattering of native tropical flowers made it briefly appear far nicer than it actually was.

As I wound through the strange labyrinth of the narrow streets, I saw a rotting yellow-and-green couch behind a spidery hanging plant on one porch. I spied three junk cars, lined up bumper to bumper, filling an entire driveway. I watched a group of small children playing in the yard of one of the houses. They stared at me as I drove slowly by. They were blond and I would have guessed all siblings, or at least related. They appeared to have been plucked out of the deep, dirty woods of Appalachia and dropped into the sandbox they had dug right into their front yard. I could see a large man standing back away from them, under the shade of a large palm tree. He had his arms crossed and stared out at me as though I were stalking his filthy children.

I maneuvered the car around one last small traffic circle. A huge clump of the dead, twisted roots of some formerly exotic tree in the middle of the circle obliterated my view of the house until I was actually there, pulling into the narrow driveway. Just as I wrestled the gearshift into "park," the sun retreated behind a line of fast-approaching clouds, confirming once and for all the tone of this odd, bleak day.

I sat for a second, paralyzed. It wasn't fear exactly; it was more like complete and utter uncertainty. There was no preparation for this. I couldn't think, "Okay, this is just like . . ." and name some other activity or task that was comparable to walking up to a depressing, shuttered house to see my dad after more than two decades. I lit a cigarette and sat there, staring at the house. Maybe they weren't home. I didn't see a car or any sign of human activity. The whole scene looked dead, still. Even the plastic whirligigs sticking out of the ground, marking the edge of a small garden of rocks, were completely motionless. It looked like a frame from a David Lynch film or a set for a Gregory Crewdson photograph.

The only thing I could think to do in this unfamiliar terrain was something equally untried. I dug into my purse and found two tubes of lipstick I had taken from my mother's dresser. I read the small round labels on the bottom of each. I decided on Frosted Hyacinth and began to apply this pink, thick material to my lips with my trembling right hand. I glared at myself in the rearview mirror, pressing my lips together. I looked like a total freak. I figured I was as ready to go see my father as I would ever be.

21

I WALKED UP the short, steep drive to the upper parking lot behind the grocery store. At the end of the parking lot there was a narrow path into a small patch of woods. I had to pull apart the wires on what was left of a fence to step through. I tossed my backpack through first then squeezed through the fence sideways. I ducked beneath a branch and around a few trees until I came to it. It was a tree that appeared to have been lifted out of the ground, slightly, so that its smooth, deformed roots were exposed, just above the dirt floor of this wooded hideout. One large root twisted around another, as though to make a braid, leaving just enough space between them for my butt. It was a perfect chair. I sat down and leaned back against the base of the tree, unzipping the side pocket of my backpack. I had just endured another hellish day of the ninth grade and was looking forward to a nice, relaxing smoke.

I could see the shining metal of the cars in the parking lot, not more than fifteen feet away. My mother's car was there. It was a rotting Honda with a bad muffler. Every day she drove it right past the service station that was one block away from the drugstore where she worked. My sister and I didn't even say anything about the car anymore. A few weeks ago I merely glanced at her as we were driving, the muffler announcing every second of our journey. She looked straight ahead and snapped, "I'll take it in when the damn thing falls off."

"Okay," I sniveled.

Some days I could see her through the trees walking to her car, fumbling through her purse for her own cigarette. I liked watching her in some sick sort of way. I could sit there smoking a cigarette, staring right at her. I found her alarming and fascinating at the same time. When she thought she was alone, she could look like the meanest, ugliest person in the world. She would talk to herself, probably repeating a conversation she had had earlier with some irate customer, someone whose order of Valium hadn't arrived. She would likely change the dialogue, turning her own inadequate words into clever, cutting quips that would leave the customer speechless as my mother turned neatly on her heel to go back to some important business, like taking inventory of mints or condoms.

This secret person inside my mother I would rather have not known about. When she was snapping at me, it seemed almost reasonable for her to be so mean. In her mind I was always in trouble, so it made sense, in a weird way, for her to act like a total bitch. But to see her nastiness just swelling up out of her for no apparent reason when she was completely alone,

Swimming

Naked

well that was just plain spooky. Her face would totally change. It would twitch and contort. She would draw in so hard on her cigarette she looked like she would suck herself right into herself. She was like Dorian Gray, only she didn't have a portrait in the attic. She had only the supposed privacy of an upper parking lot and her daily walk to her shit can of a car.

I had an hour or so to kill before Anna would notice I wasn't home from school, so I got out my journal and began to scribble my important thoughts. I had graduated from a diary at the beginning of the year when my English teacher, Mrs. Kramer, recommended we "journal." She was the only teacher I could tolerate. Under any other circumstances her enthusiasm would have made her my instant enemy. But she was wildly interested in me and what I had to say, at least on paper. I barely spoke in class. I just shoved my papers toward her and waited, secretly eager for her public cries of admiration. To keep my cover as someone who didn't give a shit, I always rolled my eyes or lowered my head as she read from my work to the class.

Mrs. Kramer's class was the only place where I came remotely close to excelling. It was very difficult to be Anna Greene's younger sister. Every teacher had already had Anna in class and each one expected me to be just like her. She had graduated from being a total nutcase to being a total suck-up. Her acting skills were put to work every day, as she convinced her teachers that she was, in the words of one of them, "an absolute angel, poor thing." She had the ability to appear both downtrodden and determined, a teenage Scarlett O'Hara, attempting to overcome her fear of every single fucking thing "as God is my witness!"

And each teacher quickly learned I had absolutely nothing in common with my sister. I didn't look like her or dress like her and I certainly didn't act like her. If they didn't recognize this right away, I made sure to clarify that I was the bad seed, the dark horse. It was easy. Slump and mumble. Wear dark clothes. Smell of cigarette smoke. Never, ever raise your hand in class except to ask to go to the bathroom. And then say, "Can I go to the bathroom?" not "May I use the rest room?" It could be subtle, rebellion, but it was important to remain steadfast to the cause at all times.

My sister and her ten to fifteen shrill and perky girlfriends from Drama Club were straight out of an episode of *Saved by the Bell*. The number of friends in her group fluctuated based on some unpredictable equation of factors including who was dating whose ex-boyfriend, who was on their period, and who had the best clothes and/or hairstyle on any given day. My two friends and I were more the *Breakfast Club* sort. We slouched mainly, dragging our feet and our sorry asses behind the building at every possible chance to smoke, our hacked up, punk-styled hair a warning for everyone to stay away. I could go weeks without uttering a single word in school. My friends, Shawna and Julie, were perfectly comfortable communicating via slight nods and the occasional, directional toss of the head. We passed copious notes to fill in the rest of the blanks, which were mostly occupied by swear words. "Can you fucking believe her? What a fucking moron.

I'll meet you after gym if I survive kickball with that fucking albino nazi lesbian basketball coach."

If you went totally by appearances, which was the code by which my mother and most every adult I knew seemed to live, my sister was perfect and I was a disaster. Plus, my sister had the extra bonus of having had a preteen nervous breakdown, so my mother was relieved every second she was practicing for a school play or shrieking over some boy rather than twirling her hair, staring blankly into space. James had a better eye for what was really going on, but he was hardly ever at home. He had taken a job at a Pittsburgh library and spent almost the whole week there. So it was back to just Anna, my mother, and me most of the time, which meant Anna and my mother, together, and me all by myself.

I tried to keep a record of these things in my journal. I wrote:

I was sitting at the table minding my own business when I heard Anna screaming into the phone in the living room, "Oh, my, God!" in her Valley Girl drawl. Anna rarely speaks in a regular voice anymore. It is hard to know what she actually sounds like.

"Men, money, and mascara. Three things you can never have enough of," she said to one of her stupid friends, as though she were some slutty twenty-year-old. She is only SIXTEEN, for God's sake. I happen to know for a fact that only two of her friends (Jana Smith and Sue "I am Perfect" Masterson) have even done it. They spend too much time looking in the mirror for fat to have sex. Besides, it wouldn't complement their fake good girl images. All the

really bad stuff they do is in secret, like smoking cigarettes AND pot, hiding booze in her makeup bottles, throwing up every meal, and that's just for starters. SHE taught ME how to smoke, thank you very much.

Anyway, my mother came in from work and looked at me with her glazed, tired stare. She rarely speaks to me and when she does she usually yells at me for some fucked up, unknown reason. She has totally given up on her Anne Romano impersonation. She doesn't even pretend to like James anymore. She asked me how school was. Like she really cares.

I could have said, "Oh, they set the cafeteria on fire today." I mumbled, "Fine." She said what she always did: "Oh, that's good." She opened another bill and said, "Goddamn heating company," then she threw the bills down on the kitchen table and left the room, stomping all the way up the stairs.

A little while later, just as I was settling into the evening, sipping on a cool, refreshing diet Coke and making my way through a bag of delicious potato chips, she shouted down to me from her room, "Lucy, when is your spring break?"

"I don't know," I yelled back, my mouth full of chips. "Ask Anna."

"How am I supposed to plan anything?" she screamed back, slamming her door. She opened it back up and yelled, "Do not yell in this house!" and slammed her door again.

Anna sighed in the next room as though the weight of the entire world had been heaved on her shoulders alone. I heard her tell Missy, Prissy, or Sissy that she had to get off the phone. She walked into the kitchen and said, "Thanks!"

"What did I do?" I asked. It was always me, somehow. She shook her head in disgust and went upstairs to my mother's room. I could hear her knock on my mother's door.

"Mom, can I come in?" she asked in her quasi-southern, perfect daughter accent. My mother let her in and soon I heard them whispering conspiratorially, laughing every so often to keep my attention. I did an experiment. I discovered if I crunched at least three chips at a time, I couldn't hear them at all and I could pretend I was completely alone. After at least half an hour of this—my crunching, their whispering—I could hear them on the steps, coming back downstairs. I grabbed the newspaper and pretended to be deeply interested in some article, oblivious to their arrival.

"Hungry, honey?" my mother asked, rubbing my head, conveniently forgetting the earlier business of yelling at me and whispering with my sister, acting like a nice mother. I decided to

I stopped to shake my hand. I had been writing so furiously I had a serious cramp. I arched my head back and stretched, yawning, then turned to look out through the trees. I could see my mother's bobbing head in the distance as she came up the hill at the other end of the parking lot. I rummaged for a cigarette. It was part of my ritual, to blow smoke right at her as she walked toward me, appearing larger and larger through the holes in the quilt of leaves.

I lit up and took a hit of smoke directly in the face, temporarily blinding myself. I shut my eyes tight, making a face. It really stung. I opened my eyes and blinked away the tears. I was startled to see my mother so close. She had walked past her car right to the edge of the woods where the path began. She had two bags of groceries in her arms and was standing completely still, staring into the woods. If she had been a couple of feet to the left, she would have been looking right at me. I froze, moving only the slightest bit to put out my cigarette, crushing it into the trunk of the tree.

She started to cry. She didn't move an inch, just clutched the overstuffed bags in her arms, her purse over her shoulder. She was crying really hard, the tears were streaming from her eyes, so much so that her cheeks and mouth were actually wet. I could see her stomach heaving between the grocery bags. But she didn't make a sound.

I turned my head and looked in the opposite direction. I sang in my head, "Mock . . . yeah! . . . ing . . . yeah! . . . bird . . . yeah! . . . yeah! . . . yeah! Mock-ing bird now everybody have you heard, he's gonna buy you . . ." It was always this odd song I pulled out of my memory to block out my unwanted thoughts about what was really happening. I would scream it in silence.

I turned back toward the parking lot. I didn't see my mother. I sat for a moment in the silence, resisting another verse of the song in my head. I heard our car start up. I listened to her drive out of the parking lot and onto the street. I could hear her as she drove toward home. I wondered if she was crying out loud now, the horrible muffler drowning out the sounds of her sobbing.

22

As soon as the door opened I had to take a step back. The dark, dank air rushed to escape the tiny house. I remembered the odor. It was Aunt Martha's place, for sure. I heard thunder in the far distance. I held my breath so I wouldn't have to smell the rotten insides of the house and to steel myself to stay removed emotionally. I was aware there was a heavy dose of ominous irony for the taking. I imagined telling the tale: "The door creaked open as the thunder began." Then I couldn't think of anyone to tell. I could feel my throat constrict and my chest burn. It was a deep and ancient pain.

"Lucy, just look at you!" Aunt Martha cried, emerging out of the darkness. She was wearing a long, burnt-red cotton robe of some sort. It had a ceremonial look to it, with hand-painted black swirls and faux-tribal emblems. She was a big woman so it was a big robe. As she moved to hug me she came into what little light was left in the overcast day. I could see she was virtually covered in cat hair. I imagined it transferring to my sun-dress, like ink to paper, as she hugged me.

"Come on in!" she welcomed. She stepped aside and bowed slightly, presenting the dark entry hall with a slow, graceful sweep of her arm, as though bidding me adieu on the yellow brick road. I didn't move an inch.

"We have missed you so much," she said, taking my arm, a gracious hostess leading me to afternoon tea.

"Your father is in the back. I thought we might catch up for a moment before we go outside," she offered.

I hadn't been able to say a word. I was still working to swal-low the sorrow lodged in my throat. I was suddenly immersed in the deep, unfathomable past, not just because of my dad, but because Aunt Martha's home was an exact replica of the apartment she had had in Cleveland years ago. It was amazing, really. I wondered if she had moved all those stacks of news-paper, the dirty dishes, the boxes and cats down here and arranged them just as one might with objets d'art and fur-niture, saying, "there, that looks perfect," placing a spaghetti-encrusted dish on top of a three-foot-tall stack of *National Geographic* magazines.

"Sit down, make yourself comfortable," she said, gesturing toward the back of the house. I made my way through the trash and began folding some fresh newspapers from the couch so I would have a place to sit.

"Oh, don't worry about that. Just put those any old place." Aunt Martha waved her hands, adopting the demeanor of a fastidious housekeeper who will suffer an out-of-place object or two in the name of hospitality. I put them on the floor, starting a new stack. Cats began to come out from around all the piles of papers and magazines. My eyes were beginning to adjust to the dark of the house. I looked around and was totally creeped out. There must have been twenty cats in this room alone. They were staring out at me from their various perches around the room. They lounged on bookshelves and TV stands. They curled up in the soil of long-dead potted plants.

"Want some coffee? I just put it on," Aunt Martha asked.

"Sure, that would be great, thanks," I said, finally getting some words around the lump in my throat. I thought hot fluid might help me somehow. Like pouring corrosive liquid down a clogged drain.

"Are you preparing for the storm?" she asked from the kitchen. I thought she was speaking metaphorically. "The hurricane is expected to hit near Miami," she clarified, adding, "They're calling it the storm of the century."

"Wow," I offered, shoving a mangy, yellow cat off my lap with one hand while wiping the frosty lipstick off my mouth with the back of my other hand.

"How is your mother?" she asked from the kitchen.

"Fine. I mean, bad. She isn't doing very well at all. The doctors don't think she'll make it more than a week or two," I answered, distracted.

I was having a hard time diverting my attention from the depressing horror of this place. There was not one window or door uncovered. I assumed that next to me, beside the couch, were sliding glass doors leading out to the back, where my father was rumored to be. It was hard to tell where light might have naturally entered the house with the thick, heavy drapes and curtains everywhere. It was easier to imagine that I was in a stranger's apartment in the slums of Russia than to believe I was here, in my aunt's disgusting, cluttered house in Florida with my dad hidden from view, behind the curtain.

"Your mother thought you might have some questions," my aunt speculated.

I looked at her, totally dumbfounded. I took a sip of the coffee she had handed to me and stared into the mug. It was the worst coffee I had ever tasted, worse than the hospital coffee.

"This must be a very difficult time for you, dear," she offered.

"You have no idea," I said, picking cat hair off my mother's sundress. I looked at the deep green drapes that separated me from my father and felt a surge of adrenaline rush through my body. My skin seemed to vibrate. I was suddenly lost somewhere between rage and panic, and the words began to tumble out of my mouth, like my body was trying to quickly heave heavy objects overboard in order to stay afloat.

"Aunt Martha, do you know we don't know anything? Not one single thing?" I began. "I didn't even know that Dad was alive at all until last week, when Mom told me he was here with you. Mom never told us anything. He just disappeared. She said he had gone and it would be best for all of us and that she knew in her heart he would be fine and we would be fine.

She said you were gone too so he was probably with you. And no offense, but that didn't give us any huge sense of security. The idea of Dad with you."

I stopped for a second. Aunt Martha was sitting perfectly still, looking at me, smiling kindly, like some sort of Earth Mother therapist. I waited for her to respond. She leaned down and picked up a nearby cat and began to stroke it, watching me, waiting for more.

I sighed and looked over at the drapes. I bit my lip and drove my fingernail into the flesh between my thumb and my hand.

"Anna has never been right. Maybe she wasn't quite right to begin with, but she has been fucked-up, really fucked-up, for a long time. She still keeps a picture of Dad under her pillow. To this day," I said, emphatically. Aunt Martha was impenetrable. She kept on stroking the cat. It was hypnotic, those strokes. I squeezed my eyes shut and opened them again.

"In fact, she probably has the picture under her pillow at the rehab clinic right now. This is her third time in rehab, you know," I accused.

"I think it was best," she said quietly, so quietly I couldn't quite understand her.

"What?" I asked.

"I think it was for the best," she repeated. "You should know your father hasn't really changed that much since you saw him last, except he's older. But we all are, aren't we?" she said, chuckling.

"He has been told just about every single thing you've

done in the past twenty years. And if there were pictures, we showed him those too," she offered, pointing to the refrigerator. "Most of them are still there. But I'm not really sure what he remembers of any of it. His memory for things seems to be pretty much gone.

"Lucy, the main thing I think you should know is that your father is quiet and gentle and kind. He was that way before and he is that way now. And that's more than I can say about most people I know." Aunt Martha tenderly placed the cat on the floor and put her hands back on her thighs. She opened her knees and leaned forward to stand up. It took some effort.

"We should go and see what your dad is up to. He was cutting the grass. I think he wanted to impress you," she said. Aunt Martha stuck her hand behind the drapes, exposing the outdoors in vertical segments. It was like waiting for the first act of the school play to commence, the curtains jerking open a few inches at a time. I could see a tiny concrete patio with huge chunks of yellow paint peeling off of it, revealing the white, grainy surface underneath. There was a cat precariously perched on a single metal chair, barely supported by the green-and-white woven plastic streamers, now shredded and dangling toward the ground.

There was a small plot of thick, springy Florida grass beyond the porch. It had just been cut. The ancient push mower had been parallel parked right next to the patio. I saw my dad at the back of the yard in the shadow of a big tree with low, curly branches. He was crouched down with his back to me, leaning over something I couldn't see.

"Frank?" Aunt Martha called out. "Lucy's here."

He didn't budge. Aunt Martha took my arm and walked me toward my dad. He was wearing a loose T-shirt, so I couldn't see if the thing was still there.

"Frank," she repeated.

We were close enough for me to see what he was looking at. It was a small, pathetic fountain, a water feature, as I had heard them advertised since arriving in Florida. It had three tiers to it, like a wedding cake; the top tier held a small cherub. My father was trying to fix the cherub, his large, hairy hand squeezing it, rotating it back and forth. He finally noticed us, Aunt Martha and me, and looked up grinning, the cherub spitting water onto the side of his face. I looked down at the ground. He was a fat old man, a moronic Arbus freak. He was a fucking fat old Lennie from *Of Mice and Men*. I started to cry.

He got up slowly, placing one hand on the ground to help him maneuver his large body up from his fountain-tending work. Aunt Martha went back into the dark house. I heard the screen door slide closed, then the glass door. She had sealed herself back in.

My dad reached for me and pulled me to his chest. I kept my arms rigid, stiff against my sides. I cried silently, tears covering my face, my chest heaving. I was afraid if I made a sound, I would never, ever stop. My dad patted my head with his hand, keeping me close to his massive chest with the other. It started to rain.

"Oh, Lucy," he said, patting my head. "It'll be okay."

That demolished me. I wrapped my arms around his back and pulled myself in close so I could smell every inch of his musty chest and neck. I began to cry even harder, releasing low primal moans. The rain wept right along with me.

Thunder rumbled loudly, not so far in the distance. The sky lit up a second later. I looked up at my dad. He was smiling, his face to the sky. He looked back down at me.

"Don't worry. I'm not afraid," he assured me.

I put my head back on his chest and he continued to pat my hair. I continued to cry, more quietly now, breathing small, irregular gasps of air in and out of my nose. I lifted my right hand and began to pat his back, gently. I didn't know if the thing was still there, hidden under his wet T-shirt, but it didn't seem to matter so much anymore. We held each other in the rain, patting to the same, slow rhythm.

23

I WENT TO open the door and was surprised to find it locked. I dug in my backpack for my house key and wondered where my mother was. She was unpredictable in too many ways to mention, but she was as punctual as they came. You could set a watch by my mother. If she got off work at 4:00 P.M., she would be home at precisely 4:25 P.M., with fifteen minutes built in to pick up milk or coffee or frozen things from the store for dinner, another five or so to walk through the lower parking lot and up the hill to her car and five to drive home. It was after 5:00 by the time I got there. I thought it was a little strange that my sister wasn't home either. I figured she must have been visiting one of her disgusting friends, painting her toenails in some girl's puffy white bedroom while discussing someone else's fat thighs.

"Hello!" I yelled, just to clarify I was indeed home alone. The echo seemed to rattle the ice maker enough to drop a few cubes. I jumped, spooked. I was usually the last one to enter the house at the end of the day and I missed the comforting sounds of the TV in my mom's room and my sister's yakity yakking on the phone. I liked things to be the same, even if they were the same depressing and stupid things. I even felt a peculiar feeling of relief when James was home and he and my mother sat in the kitchen together, their faces filled with hate. At least they were there. I would hover around them, taking forever to find a snack or make a sandwich. After a while my mother would say, "Lucy, James and I were talking." I would act surprised and fumble around some more before leaving them, making a big scene out of trying to carry a plate and a glass and a napkin out of the kitchen so they could resume their silent conversation.

I called out once more just to be sure. "Anna? Mom?"

I could hear the house quietly humming to me that no one was home. I went up the wooden stairs, slowly, listening carefully to each and every creak and moan. My mother had hung pictures all the way up the stairs. I stopped to look at each of them. It was our family album, but like our family history, it had a selective memory. There was Anna, an infant, staring out of the mesh side of a playpen, one wild curl on top of her head, her eyes wide. There was Anna and me, sitting on the concrete front steps of a house that I didn't recognize. We were eating Popsicles, the photo snapped midlick. We were in bathing suits and our hair was wet. There was a picture of my mother and some of her stewardess friends at a fancy bar in New York. She was wearing a slinky black dress and a diamond sort of necklace. Her hair was up in a very high twist. She was smoking and laughing, looking off in the distance. It was no wonder she framed that picture. She looked like Audrey Hepburn. There were a handful more of my sister and me. They looked as though they were all taken on the same summer day at the house I couldn't remember. They had a brownish yellow cast to them, as though pissed upon by time.

Every single remaining photograph, a good seventy-five percent of them, was taken in the last five years. The James years. These all had a bluish green tint to them, cheerfully surreal. There must have been at least fifteen from Cape Cod, the theme of which all seemed to be "Let's Make a Muscle!" There was a picture of James and my mother at some library conference. James was very shiny and red and looked unusually sheepish. My mother was gazing up at him and looked unusually adoring. She had one hand on the back of his head. This was an early photo from the James years.

The last one was my favorite. James had taken it and had been the one to frame it and add it to the wall. My mother hated it. We were standing in front of a redbrick wall. It was actually the side of an Italian restaurant near our house. One night we had gone for dinner to pretend we were still a happy family. James had just bought a new camera, a fancy 35mm one for his artsy black-and-white photographs. He said he wanted to snap us in the last light of the day. Golden hour he called it. We stood against the wall as he fussed with the camera for what seemed like an eternity. He must have taken several shots of us before we officially posed. In this one, my mother was leaning against the wall in profile, looking to the left side of the frame, scowling. Her cigarette dangled from her limp hand in front of her. My sister was hugging my mother from behind, her hands around my mother's waist, her head leaning against my mother's neck with her face looking toward the camera. Her eyes were closed and she had the softest, sweetest smile. I was standing with my back against the wall, looking up to the sky with my hands extended out, palms up. I had thought I felt a raindrop and was feeling for more. It looked as though I were begging for divine intervention, praying it would come fast and take me then and there, away from my mother and my sister.

I was pondering this last picture when I heard a loud noise upstairs. I was so startled I screamed. I was even more startled to hear a scream in return. I started to run down the steps, screaming, and got halfway to the front door before I realized that it was just my sister and I, screaming at the top of our lungs, freaking each other out. She must have had the same revelation at about the same time. We were both silent, then yelled each other's names in angry unison. I stomped back up the stairs and shoved her slightly opened door so hard it slammed into the wall behind it.

"Jesus Christ, Anna. Why didn't you say you were home?" I yelled at the back of her head. She was sitting on the other side of her bed on the floor, facing the wall. She didn't answer me.

"Anna, what are you doing?" I asked, coming around the bed so I could see her.

She looked up at me, her cheeks streaked with tears and mascara, like black rivers running straight into the gutter. She was smoking a cigarette, using a jar of cold cream for an ashtray. She had a whole bottle of our mother's wine next to her and took a huge gulp of it straight out of the bottle. "I had a rough day," she explained, taking another drink. "Here," she said, flinging the bottle toward me like it was a baton in a relay race, then grabbing it back like I was trying to steal it from her.

"Have a seat," she said, patting the floor beside her with her other hand. She took another drink.

Something big was up. That was for sure. First my mother was sobbing in the parking lot and now my sister was drunk in the afternoon, looking a total mess. I suddenly seemed very well adjusted. I sat down next to my sister and lit a cigarette. I took the bottle from her and took a big drink. It was warm and fruity and terrible. I took another drink.

Anna's curling iron and hot roller hairdo had come completely undone. Her curls were springing up this way and that. She looked like Little Orphan Annie on smack. She started rocking back and forth to complete the image for me. She was jonesing for something. I handed her the bottle.

"So . . . ," I began, not quite sure where to go with this business of hanging out with my sister.

"So!" she accused. "So goddamn what?" she cried. It occurred to me that she had reached the edge of her anger, saying the worst thing she could get out of her mouth. It also occurred to me that *fuck* was a much stronger word, vocabulary-wise. It was a switch-hitting word and could play as a verb, noun, adjective—you name it. I hoped in time Anna would come to love and admire *fuck* as much as I did.

"Yeah, fuck, I mean, really," I replied shaking my head slowly back and forth, commiserating and illustrating a point, all at the same time.

"You don't know anything," Anna accused, handing me the bottle.

"I do too!" I retorted.

"Do you know that James isn't coming back?" she spit, crying even harder.

"Yes," I lied. "I figured." My head was spinning. I had the taste of dead grapes and ashes in my mouth and my stomach was burning. James wasn't coming back. James wasn't coming back. James wasn't coming back. There's no place like home. There's no place like home. There's no place like home. I could hear my sister's voice cutting through the swirl of unintelligible words in my head.

"They're getting a divorce as soon as possible. Mom talked to him today," she explained, moving her hand to my knee and patting it as though to console me.

"How do you know?" I was having a hard time following all of this.

"Mom came home right before you did and told me. She's driving to Pittsburgh right this minute. Why? I have no idea," Anna said, taking the bottle back from me, lighting another cigarette. She fished into the cold cream around the ashes and cigarettes and began to smooth some of it onto her mascara-streaked cheeks. It looked like she was finger painting on her face.

"What's she going to do when she gets there?" I asked. Before Anna could answer I started laughing hysterically.

"What?" she asked, her briefly misplaced disdain for me now present and accounted for.

I couldn't explain. It was so funny, the idea in my head. I fell into Anna's lap, and tried to share the joke with her.

"He'll hear her coming from miles away, with her loud, stupid car. And he'll run for the hills. And he'll never be seen again," I stuttered, between fits of laughter. "Just like Dad!" I concluded, laughing even harder.

When I stopped laughing, when I got tired of imagining my mother chasing them away, first my father and then James, I looked up at my sister and reconsidered; maybe it was her fault. With her wild hair and crazy eyes, her white skin under her gray finger-painted face, she sure looked like the living dead, a siren gone real bad, a dead fucking duck. Who would want to live with her?

"I'm going to go live with James," I declared.

"He doesn't want you," Anna slurred. "Mom says he doesn't want any of us."

"Well, I don't want to live with any of you!" I shouted through my tears. "I don't want to live with you or Mom or James!" I grabbed the bottle from her and drank. I wouldn't look at her as she rubbed my back. I kept crying as she smoothed my hair, combing it away from my face with her fingers. As much as I desired tenderness, it made me feel infinitely more miserable.

So we kept drinking. We drank until Anna threw up. This time I held her hair back, pulling on it too hard, adding to her misery as I stood behind her over the toilet, weaving. Then we stumbled to her bed and passed out. When we woke up in the morning, fully clothed and entwined like lovers, we jumped up quickly, blaming the wine. My mother showed up a few hours later, looking as wretched as we did. She took down nearly all the photos from the stairwell, removing all the James photos from the archive and leaving only the earliest piss-stained records of a day I don't even remember.

True to form, we never spoke of James in that house again.

24

I ARRIVED BACK at the hospital a little before dark. The asphalt parking lot was sparsely populated, which seemed odd given the time of day. I emerged from the car and peeled my clothes away from my body, the sweat of the cross-state drive having turned the cotton sundress into black Saran Wrap. I rustled the skirt of the dress, trying to drum up some sort of a breeze on my legs. It was noticeably still. I rummaged in the car for a napkin and found one that hadn't captured falling gobs of special sauce from my hold-the-onion Big Mac. I used it to mop up under my arms. I glanced around for witnesses before wiping the sweat between my legs.

I lit a cigarette to get my nicotine levels up even higher for the hospital and sat precariously on the edge of the rear bumper, trying to keep any exposed skin from coming into contact with the car. It was ridiculously hot. I studied the fingernails of my left hand. I had been trying with all my might for the past four hours to avoid thinking about my father, my mother, my sister—all of them. I had found deeply interesting information on overhead exit signs, the backs of semi trucks, and billboards. When signage failed to further intrigue me, I tried to determine how long it would take me to arrive at my destination if I dropped my speed by one mile each time I drove one mile closer to where I was going. That proved far too hard for a right-brained girl so I decided to chain-smoke instead. So I did. Right into the hospital parking lot. When I heard someone calling my name I was pretty sure my hiatus was coming to an abrupt and bitter end.

"Oh there you are, thank God," Bella called out, walking toward me as quickly as she was able. This fast pace of hers wasn't really fast at all. She seemed to be slowed by an oblique rocking motion, the side-to-side gate of the overweight. I stepped on my cigarette and stood to face her. I prayed she wouldn't hug me.

"Dear, you should come with me. Your mother isn't doing so well and the doctors are eager to speak to you," she explained, between gasps. She had clearly overexerted herself. She put one hand to her chest, as though to steady her heart. "I'm so sorry you have to deal with all of this at one time, but you must." With that, she took my arm and led me toward the emergency room entrance. My sandals stuck to the asphalt at each step as if they had a light film of glue covering the soles.

"Oh, my, what a day," Bella declared with a sigh. "You see your father, you drive so far, your mother, the hurricane. It is too much."

We had just entered the strangely lit refrigeration unit called the ER. I was having a hard time processing information. I had become quite enamored with the uncomplicated mental landscape of the open road and my fingernails. And to be perfectly honest, I had taken two of my mother's painkillers about halfway across the state of Florida. There was a low, pleasant hum in my ears and a slight tingle all over my body, a little night music and a postorgasmic murmur in my skin. So what if it was chemically induced? I stopped at a drinking fountain and took a long, greedy drink. When I stood back up I recalled Bella's words.

"A hurricane," I repeated, as though learning the English language. This sounded familiar to me, although it was as clear a day as I had seen since I had been down there. There wasn't even the slightest breeze.

"Hurricane Pierre. It's supposed to hit land by tomorrow night. And right now it is headed pretty much straight toward us. It's a big one," Bella explained, punching the up button on the elevator repeatedly. She seemed to be in a really big hurry. "We have to see the doctors and we have to get ready for the storm," she said, explaining her rush.

I was stuck on the hurricane. Not its imminent arrival or reported ferocity or the preparations she implied we would have to make to greet it. I was baffled by its pretentious French name.

"Isn't that a weird name for a hurricane?" I asked. She looked at me askance, both baffled and concerned. Then she took my arm and pulled me into the elevator.

"Lucy, your mom has gone downhill considerably since yesterday."

I looked at the numbers lighting up as we ascended. Two. Three. Four. Five.

"Lucy," Bella snapped.

"Hmm?" I asked.

The elevator doors opened on six, the top floor of the hospital. We walked toward the nursing station in the middle of the floor. We were still quite a distance from the station when Bella called out, "She's here. I found her." We both got disapproving looks from the two nurses who were standing there. I made a face right back at them.

"I'll get the doctor," Nurse Ratchet droned.

I was freezing. All my sweat had turned into an icy epidermal layer, a second skin. I had the idea that my mother was probably just freezing to death. But when I entered her room, the third on the left past the nurses' station, I thought otherwise. I was slapped out of my drug fog into a reality I was not at all ready to face. My mother was dying right in front of my eyes.

She had been dying since I came here. But somehow, in one day, she turned the corner from some sappy metaphoric or even terminally ill death state and started to die in earnest. From all the way across the room I could see it. I could feel it. I could smell it. She had shrunk even more and had become notably smaller overnight. She threw off a death scent like a cheap drugstore perfume. I walked closer to her bed.

Her brow was creased and her shrunken head moved slowly

side to side. Deep moans escaped her lips. It was clear she was not comfortable at all. She had come no further toward a sense of peace with dying and her distress was evident. I could see the pain ripple across the sharp planes of her body. It looked as though she wanted to move away from it but was too weak to do so. Her body was at war with itself and you could see the battlefield just beneath her translucent skin: a bomb exploding below her neck; a squadron of young, excitable soldiers running up her thigh.

She was skeletal and her hair looked dead already. It was hair as it is generally rendered in the living dead, zombie films. There were random tufts of thin, dreary dental floss–like strands sprouting out from her scaly head. She had lost so much weight her skin rested in soft, wrinkled folds against her face, her neck, her arms. She was ashen and green. There was no flattering light, no alluring position. There was no dignity in this for her. I don't care what anyone said.

"I have been giving her massage," Bella told me, from the doorway.

"That's good," I responded, staring at the wreck of a woman on the bed in front of me.

"It will make her more relaxed for the end," Bella said. "It would be good if you could massage her too," she suggested.

The nurses have been encouraging me to touch her since I got here. They wanted me to comb what was left of her hair and rub her back. They wanted me to give her a sponge bath. I've done her hair. That's it. And I hold her hand. I connect the dots with her age spots. I pretend they are stars and make constellations out of them. I think of it as our thing, my mother's and mine; our one and only thing. I simply cannot touch her anywhere else. I am terrified of her bones and her veins.

I am terrified.

25

I HADN'T EVEN completed half the circle of the circular driveway when I knew it was all a big mistake. Anna's house looked terrible, and not in the run-down, lived-in, rough-around-the-edges style I was used to. I preferred good houses that had fallen on hard times, Victorians with sloping porches and Tudors with crumbling brick. This was a bad house: the evidence of a good economy, a doctor's salary, and my sister's taste, informed by Disney in the early years and *Town & Country* magazine of late. Just by looking at the outside, a giant stone edifice of some ambiguous architectural style, I would have bet money, big money, that chintz and stencils were to play a major role in the decor.

I was a snob, to be sure. I had spent the last four years moving toward a degree in art history at Case Western Reserve University in Cleveland. I was a good enough student, which was a bit of a surprise to everyone, including myself. The only

reason I got in the school in the first place, with a scholar-
ship no less, was because of my freakishly high SAT scores.
Several of my professors believed I had considerable talent for
critical evaluation. I didn't let on I had been in training for
such a thing my entire life. One of the professors whom I
had charmed but with whom I had not had sex became my
adviser and mentor. Her name was Laura Steele. At first I
thought her to be humorless. Later I discovered otherwise. It
was just that she was the first person to speak to me without
any trace of sarcasm, ever. I sought her company often and
served as her assistant for two years. When I first started
working for her, I would try out a statement I had heard in a
bar, at a coffeehouse, in class, or, more likely, in someone's
bed. I was always on the lookout for the truth but was not a
natural scout.

"Your friends sound interesting. Gullible perhaps, but earnest," Dr. Steele would say quietly. She always listened without
judgment to my stories of recklessness disguised as freedom. I
told her stories about my life as though I were whispering into
a canyon, wondering if it might sound different as the words
bounced off of something, someone, and headed back my
way. She would rarely respond with words. She might nod or
go "hmm." Once I told her a particularly sad little tale of waking up naked in a strange, filthy bed with a man I did not
know. I told the story with bravado and humor, as though saying good-bye to a man whom you have fucked but whose
name you do not know, stumbling out of his unfamiliar house,
into an unfamiliar neighborhood, with no money and no car

in the middle of the night is a hilarious thing. She looked at me for a long time and finally said, "I would think that would feel terrible. All of it." I thought I was going to throw up, right there in her office. The truth can be sickening when it is your own.

I had decided to take my spring break and drive to Cincinnati to see Dr. and Mrs. George Bellows and their not-so-new baby, Sarah Elizabeth, whom I had seen only once in her life, at a christening in February of the year before. I was homesick for something, anything that felt like family, even if that meant Anna. My mother had remarried again, eloped actually, and was living in Nebraska or some ridiculous state like that. She sent me a letter and photo right after the school year began to announce the nuptials and to forward an address. The blessed union occurred in Las Vegas. "A riot!" wrote my mother. "So trashy!"

She had enclosed a wedding portrait, taken after she married Ron Davidson. It was nighttime in Vegas and someone had taken their picture outside the chapel. Ron was standing behind my mother and had his arms around her in a bear hug, lifting her off the ground in some sort of big-time wrestling move. I suspect he picked this up in the military, from which he had just retired from an entire lifetime of professional duty. His friends, and now my mother, called him Red Dog. "I don't know why," penned my ever-curious mother. She was careening down a brand-new path of odd behavior, her ass packed in a pair of stonewashed jeans, an ankle bracelet below. She was wearing bad shoes, as usual, this time a reddish brown pair of scuffed-up pumps. Her hair was seriously frosted and feathered, shoulder length. I couldn't make out the words on her T-shirt.

She was oddly intimate in her letter, like she had confused me with a college chum from another era. She wrote she was outside by the pool. Red Dog was taking a nap. I could imagine her there, sitting at a white metal table with a worn umbrella beside the tiny motel pool, close to the cement path that led to the rooms, near the humming ice machine. She would look up when the machine dropped some cubes or when the extremely tan woman in the pool shrieked as her boyfriend, also very tan, slipped his hand down her swimsuit. The rest of the time she would be diligently writing her letter, telling me far too much about "how little sleep she gets with Red Dog around, if you know what I mean." She went on to say how she decided to try the pill, hoping her "you-know-whats get bigger." As much as I enjoyed torturing my sister, I prayed she didn't receive a similar letter. Anna continued to revere my mother for reasons unknown to me. I was certain she would be very disturbed by my mother's impersonation of a sexually knowing, slightly naughty, fun-loving woman.

I had just stopped the car when I saw Anna. She came around the house from the side yard, leaning on a stick or cane of some sort. She brought her limping self to a stop and leaned on her walking stick and waved, with one arm raised high, as though hailing a rescue plane. I waved back, a tiny little wiggle of my fingers, turned off the ignition, and took a deep breath.

26

I GRABBED a small bottle of water out of the cooler near the front of the glowing Wal-Mart. After watching Bella wringing her hands by the window for an hour, I finally got it out of her that she was less worried at that very moment about my mother's passing than she was about returning to her condominium and finding it without electricity and water. She was quite certain the hurricane would come and rob her of these creature comforts for a few days. She was also certain that her home, her tiny condo, would be intact without any major damage. She was equally convinced this would be the exact same fate of my mother's condo. I allowed myself to lean into her optimism for support since I had run out of the little I had to begin with. We decided she should stay and I should go. It was easy. I was the only one who could drive. I tried not to appear eager but I was ecstatic for an errand, to be asked only to buy some things on a list. I left the hospital with a pager in

176

one pocket and Bella's hurricane shopping list in the other. I walked by the nurses' station. They were split this time in their regard for me; Eileen, the one I liked, gave me a sympathetic smile, the other a heavy sigh.

I stopped and walked back and slammed my hands down on the desk, startling them both. "Can I get you anything at the Wal-Mart?" I asked, directing my super-bitch glare to the sighing, beleaguered one. She looked up at me and pressed her lips together as though to keep her judgmental thoughts from spilling out and over the counter. I hated her guts. I hated every inch of her puffy, out-of-shape body that she had stuffed into her white stretchy uniform and her white stockings and her white shoes. I hated her oversized red-framed glasses and her thinning, permed hair. I wanted to punch her in her paunchy, middle-aged, polyester-encased stomach.

"Do you think I want to go to Wal-Mart to buy hurricane supplies? Do you think I want to come back here and watch my mother die? Do you think I want to be here in your stupid hospital at all? Do you think that *I* would be in fucking *Florida* unless I had to?" I ranted.

She looked down at the charts on the desk. I remembered the technique. I had used it with my mother. She was hoping that if she remained motionless, I might just move on. Once I was gone she would look up, clear her throat, and go back to her work, basically unscathed. She would feel justified in her judgments of me. I had proven her right with my yelling and carrying on. My anger was making me feel sick so I left without doing any further harm. When I was at the end of the hall by the elevator, I heard her cough one quiet, raspy cough. I stabbed the down button with my finger.

I had driven over to the Wal-Mart on nearly empty streets. According to the radio, they had been evacuating everyone within a mile of the coast all day long. I drove fast, suddenly enjoying my mother's big-ass car in this tropical ghost town. It was starting to rain, just a little bit; the first harbinger of fussy Hurricane Pierre, the supposed *mère* of all storms. Bella had unleashed a torrent of Hurricane Pierre information once we had decided that I would be going out for provisions. Her predictions sounded suspiciously like the doctors' regarding my mother's death. Both my mother's death and Hurricane Pierre were hovering just off the coast. Both were expected to arrive within twenty-four hours. And it was anticipated that both would hit hard and do lasting, even irreparable damage. Pierre had a slight chance of veering off on a sudden, unexpected northerly excursion, missing the mark entirely. I suspected my mother's death was a more precise storm, on an inexorable course. I had driven even faster, wishing I had some more painkillers. I could find only two dirty Tylenols at the bottom of my purse. I washed them down with the water from the Wal-Mart cooler and grabbed a shopping cart.

"We're closing in two hours!" a uniformed boy shouted at me, shoving carts into each other. Their huge plastic frames made an unsatisfying, hollow noise as each humped the next in line. Mine squeaked and lurched its way in front of me just like its metal cousin might, the plastic innovation apparently providing no solution to the common, everyday cart problem:

the aberrant wheel. Who could shop in one store for two hours? I had never been in a Wal-Mart. I shoved the cart past the speedy photo-processing mini-store and into the bowels of the mega-store. I nearly cried. I had entered shopping hell.

It was a mile long by a half-mile deep of brightly colored crap. If the ceiling were any lower, it would have felt like a giant shopping coffin. I grabbed a neon green sweater off a circular rack crammed with colorful cotton garments and put it on. I was still in my mother's sundress and it was freezing in here. I stopped for a split second to make sure I was hearing the music correctly. I laughed out loud. It was a Muzak version of "These Boots Are Made for Walkin'." The Wal-Mart top brass were employing the same tactics as the FBI at Waco, Texas! They were going to freeze me out of their store or make me insane from the music! I would become discombobulated and quickly buy a few hundred bucks' worth of junk, pay up, and then run toward the interior of Florida, away from Hurricane Pierre! It was a clever plan. I pushed on, outwitting them, my cart's wheel squeaking along to "Boots, get walkin'."

I set my purse on the kid seat/purse ledge of the shopping cart and dug inside for the list. I spied the pager and picked it up. I looked at the tiny screen on which some sort of message would appear. I had never used a pager and didn't know what would happen, exactly, if and when I was paged. I put it in the handy pocket of my green Wal-Mart cardigan. I squeaked and lurched on.

The store was so huge that it was impossible to know how

to navigate for efficient shopping. I suspected this was not an accident. I was looking for double quantities of batteries, flashlight, canned goods, first-aid kit, water, battery-operated radio, crossword puzzle. I guessed the puzzle was Bella's choice for entertainment during the aftermath of the storm. I was hoping to fly the fuck out of Florida and entertain myself with an in-flight shopping magazine, imagining myself purchasing virtual-reality goggles and a chair that massaged every inch of me. I was looking forward to being the girl on the plane who makes all the passengers roll their eyes or shake their heads, sad for me in my vulgar and drunken state. I would lean over to one of them across the aisle, my finger stirring my fourth Bloody Mary. In the forward cycle of my drunken rocking motion I would stop suddenly, my head jerking forward then back. I would blink slowly then confess in a loud stage whisper, "My mother died in the storm."

My cart came to a halt. The wheel was so turned around it wanted to move in a direction other than the way I had intended. I took it as a sign from God and moved toward automotive supplies rather than the garden center. My shopping plan was not as precise as my escape-from-Florida plan. The grid of the store seemed to allow for aisle-stocking devices on which special seasonal things might be placed. I imagined all the Back-to-School merchandise had been held at bay while they ran around throwing storm things together. Someone had made a frantic call to Wal-Mart Central, where batteries, flashlights, and the like were aplenty. "We need the truck here yesterday!" the assistant manager would have screamed into the phone, slamming it down to march around the store. The attempt was to look busy, powerful, purposeful. The result was to look harried and out of control. Shoppers became nervous, throwing even odder combinations of merchandise into their carts. Batteries and flashlights plus a *People* magazine and bath beads and some toilet cleanser. All in all, the Wal-Mart system was foolproof. No matter what happened to you in the store, you were moved to buy things you neither wanted nor needed.

I spotted a couple of small, red plastic flashlights. I was hoping for the long, silver night watchman's kind. I grabbed two of the plastic ones. There were only five of these and there were a handful of customers rushing about the store with their own lists. I wasn't up for a fight of that sort, the grabbing and elbowing kind. Cleverly located on the next storage device were batteries. At first glance it appeared the C battery stock was entirely depleted. I panicked a bit. Then I slowly scanned every battery package, knowing that my keen eye could find at least two packages of C batteries. It wasn't my curatorial eye that would help me here. My training was in stockings. I was a woman who on occasion, believe it or not, needed to procure one pair of size B, nude or black stockings. No control top. No reinforced toe. And no easy task. So I employed the same foolproof system. I would start top left and scan and shuffle through each package, ignoring the signage that was of no use whatsoever. I would breathe through my anger.

I found them. One package was among a heap of triple A's that had fallen to the floor. The other was hidden behind a bunch of nine-volt batteries. I was momentarily elated. I stood up and looked ahead of me and was instantly defeated. It was a sea of consumer goods, a maze of plastic and nylon and vinyl and rubber and cardboard. I had been here for nearly an hour and I only had two stupid things from the list. And as hard as I had been trying, I couldn't forget my mother.

To remind me just how serious all this was, the pager made a noise, a double beep, a puny alarm bell deep in my pocket. It was vibrating as well. I looked at the little, horizontal screen and saw a phone number on it. It was the only Florida phone number I knew by heart. It was the nursing station at the hospital.

I looked up and saw the young boy who had alerted me to the closing time at the beginning of my shopping adventure. He was coming toward me with long, purposeful strides. He was a confident worker. I must have looked as bewildered and lost as I felt. He stopped and asked me if I needed any help.

I stared at my list, now crumpled in my left hand. I stared at the pager in my right. I looked inside my cart. The flash-lights and the batteries appeared as small and insignificant as the cars, homes, driveways, and swimming pools of a suburb, seen while looking out the window of an ascending airplane.

"My mother's dying and I need these things," I told him, unable to separate the thoughts, to place priority on one thing over the other.

Tears sprang to his eyes. He looked as though I had told him the worst thing in the whole world. It occurred to me then and there, for the very first time, that perhaps it was.

"I'll help you," he said, taking the list from my hand. It was as chivalrous and courageous a gesture as I had ever seen. I had to look away as he strode off with my squeaking cart in search of provisions for my emergency.

I thought I should find a pay phone to call the hospital, but I didn't know what they might tell me that could have any influence over my next steps. The boy would come back with my things and I would buy them then drive back to the hospital. I couldn't make things go any faster on my end or slower on my mother's. So I put the pager back in my pocket and I stood there, in the middle of the Wal-Mart, my hands at my sides, empty. I had nothing to hold on to anymore. I looked at the backs of my hands. I turned them over and looked at the palms. I wondered which of the deep, crisscrossed lines were the ones that foretold my sister the drunk, my father the freak, my mother dead at age fifty-eight. I began to trace made-up patterns using my left finger to navigate the maze of my life, as told in the palm of my right hand. I closed my eyes and pointed, imagining I would find the single intersection, the palmistry constellation, that anticipated this moment in time where I would go sit by my mother and watch her die. I wondered if a real palm reader could have known and told me in advance how completely unprepared and unqualified I was for such a task.

I heard the squeak of a cart behind me. I turned to see the boy practically running with my cart, now almost full with all that was on the list. I imagined he was better prepared than I was. He would know what to do. He slowed down and pushed the cart toward the line. I followed him. He stood

Swimming

Naked

there, silently, looking straight ahead, his hands on the cart, waiting for it to be our turn, my turn to check out.

"My mother is at home," he said quietly. "She isn't afraid of the hurricane. I'm not either," he assured himself.

I barely heard him. I was staring at a package that was hanging amid the lighters, barrettes, combs, and fingernail clippers, the seemingly universal assortment of items available right at checkout. It was adjacent to the hairnets, the package of glow-in-the-dark stars. The stars were a yellowish fluorescent color and came in varying sizes, from dime-sized little stars to stars as big as silver dollars. I grabbed the package and clutched it to my chest. I was suddenly in a hurry to get back to my mother.

I turned to thank the boy. He was gone. I hoped he was going home to his mother. I hoped they would brave the storm together. I hoped at one particularly windy moment, when a quickly nailed shutter blew off the window and banged across the roof, they would hug each other tight, showing for at least one second how afraid they really were.

STACY

SIMS

27

As soon as Anna's limp and walking stick had fully registered, I noticed she was wearing a disturbing outfit. She had
on a white blouse with a Peter Pan collar underneath a pink,
crewneck sweater with a strand of pearls barely visible along
the neckline of the blouse. Her pink-and-kelly-green-plaid
wool shorts were cuffed just above her knees, practically graz-
ing the tops of her white kneesocks. Penny loafers with actual
pennies in them finished the ensemble. She had her hair
pulled back away from her face in a ponytail and topped that
off with a headband adorned with green, pink, and white ribbon. Every single inch of her body had been considered. Her
nails were painted; her wedding and engagement rings sparkled.
A gold watch with tiny diamonds around the face peeked out
from the edge of the crisp cuff of her blouse. A gold-and-
diamond tennis bracelet rested against the opposing cuff, the

second half of a twinset of sorts. She was fully made up, wearing pink lipstick that matched the color of her sweater exactly. Even her walking stick had a subtle green painted in the grooves of its carved handle.

"Well, hello, stranger," she said as she walked toward me. She leaned the walking stick against the front of my car and hobbled the next three steps to greet me, like a paraplegic bravely taking her first heroic steps. Before I could say a word she had her hands on my shoulders and was pulling me in for an embrace, kissing my right check, *mmwoa,* and then the left, *mmwoa.* She smiled. She was twenty-four years old going on forty-seven. She took a step back, staggered a bit, and reached for her walking stick. Once she had regained her balance, she used her free hand to sweep a few invisible strands of hair even closer to her head, shoring up her composure. She settled her shoulders back into their most correct possible posture and sighed, wearily. It seemed this two-minute greeting had taken every ounce of strength she could muster.

"Let's go in. Come on! You must be exhausted," she said, turning, cane and all, with military precision. She kept talking, suddenly recovered from her moment of lethargy, and limped quickly to her front door. "Just leave your bags. Natalia will get them. Or George. Everyone is out, so we have some time to get caught up. Or maybe you want to take a nap."

I still hadn't spoken a word. This was a lot to take in all at once. I mustered a noncommittal "well, okay" before reaching inside the front seat of the car for my purse. I quickly stuffed all of its contents, which had been dug out and littered on the passenger seat in an earlier attempt to find a mint, back inside my bag. I grabbed the cigarettes last, squeezing the pack to ascertain, approximately, how many smokes were left. It felt to be a dismal three or four, for all practical purposes an empty pack. I wanted to get right back in the car for a backup supply, but it occurred to me that it might not be a bad thing at all to have to go out to the store in an hour or so.

When we first walked into the foyer, she moved to the epicenter of the two-story entrance hall and turned to face me, like Vanna White. The floor was marked, like a stage, by the center ring of a contemporary deep purple rug with dark green spirals. The rug must have been fifteen feet in diameter and was flanked by twin marble-topped tables. Huge slabs of green marble rested on black, shiny, round wooden pedestals, two each per table. On top of each table sat identical vases with identical floral arrangements. The vases had a faux Oriental look to them and the flowers, more appropriate for a hotel lobby, were arranged with such symmetry that it took the wind right out of their exotic sails. The end of the room featured two floor-to-ceiling windows. Precisely where you would have hoped a door to be was a plantation-style armoire, at least seven feet tall. The armoire had the same black shiny veneer as the pedestals. It should have been old but was brand-new. Everything looked to have cost a fortune, but nothing appeared to have any lasting value. It was an expensive set for my sister's lavish, nouveau revival of "Wealthy Suburban Housewife."

Anna stood silently for a brief moment as I gaped at the

entrance to her home. She interpreted my own silence as reverent awe and launched into what can best be described as a song-and-dance routine, only without the song and dance. Anna talked nonstop for a solid hour. The only time she seemed to breathe was when she came up for air, a literal ascension of her upper body, after doubling over in laughter at her own tired jokes. There was a nervous trill barely perceptible under her words, a tenuousness that would be hard to detect through her cover of a remarkable barrage of words. She also had a slight facial tic. She had replaced twirling her hair with her finger with a lightning fast pucker of her mouth and an occasional furrow of the brow. This too was such a quick gesture it appeared to be more of a twitch than a purposeful look of dismay. The other notable feat was that Anna did not sit still for more than a second. Even with her injury, which I had yet to hear about, she was constantly on the move.

After the tour of all four bedrooms, three full and two half baths, the sewing room, laundry room, den, living room, and sunroom, we finally landed in the kitchen, an all-white homage to excessive cleanliness. Anna was rattling on about a dinner party she had thrown between Christmas and New Year's. "A perfect time, really, to do something totally outrageous with food. Everyone is so sick of the traditional holiday fare," Anna explained.

She continued as though firing words from a machine gun, "So I decided to do a Mexican-themed party. We had these real Mexicans cooking chicken and steak for fajitas and a margarita stand set up in the sunroom. I had a piñata specially ordered. It was my idea to fill it with individually wrapped Godiva chocolates, for dessert. Everyone loved that part. George broke the piñata after nearly wiping out both vases in the entry." Anna shook her head slowly; a wry smile indicated she could see it all as plain as day. She laughed. It was a dry and fatigued chuckle.

"I had a few too many margaritas and George ended up furious with me."

The story was beginning to get interesting so I rescued my cigarettes from my back pocket and dug for the lighter in the pack. We had spent our high school and college years commiserating on the ridiculous behavior of men, particularly those with whom we were involved. After James left we forged a friendship of sorts, in secret. When we were in public, we acted either oblivious or disdainful of the other's presence. But in the privacy of our home or over the phone when she went to college, we trashed men. No one was spared. Certainly not boyfriends nor her husband.

I was sitting at one of two white kitchen stools and happily lit up, my elbows atop the white laminate countertop of the breakfast island. Anna, who had taught me to smoke when I was fourteen, stood away from the sink, against which she had been leaning, and reprimanded me.

"Oh, for God's sake, Lucy," she said, practically spitting her words. "I am married to a doctor and have a young child in the house. Don't you think it is a bit presumptuous to smoke in the house? Go outside, if you must."

I got off my stool and began to walk toward the sunroom,

off of which was a wooden, multitiered deck leading down to a perfectly manicured and never-used lawn. I turned before I reached the door.

"Anna, a year ago you were married to a doctor and had an even younger child and we smoked a carton of cigarettes between the two of us, indoors, in roughly three days. I'll smoke outside, but don't be such a fucking prima donna." I immediately felt bad and started to say something apologetic when I saw her mouth pucker and her brow twitch, simultaneously.

"Please do not say 'fuck' in this house either," she snapped.

"Oh, brother," I said, and quietly concluded "fuck" as I slid the door closed. I decided it seemed a good time to head to the gas station for more cigarettes. I wanted to drive around and smoke my brains out for a half hour or so until I had to reenter Anna's bizarre sanctuary. I stamped out my cigarette on the deck, making a graffiti pattern with the ash. I kicked the butt over the edge, sending it to rest somewhere below, where some poor migrant gardener, perhaps a *real* Mexican, would have to pick it out of the mulch.

"I've got to run out for a minute," I called to my sister as I looked for where she might have hidden my purse, an object that might clutter any one of the pristine rooms. "Where did you put my purse?" I called again. "Anna?" I said in the direction of the kitchen. I realized she wasn't in the kitchen, nor did she appear to be downstairs at all. I started up the stairs and called again, "Anna, where are you? I need to get my purse and run out for a second."

As I moved up the stairs, lights turned on to automatically

highlight my path. With all the windows and skylights in the house, the stairways and interior halls were surprisingly dark. They created protracted, winding distances between the spaces where people dwelled. I thought of Sarah Elizabeth and imagined that once she was able to walk, it would be a long, terrifying journey in the middle of the night from her room to her parents' room, fancy automatic lights and all.

"Anna?" I called again, beginning to feel concerned.

I heard something from one of the upstairs rooms. I followed the sound, which I couldn't quite make out, and entered the guest room, my chintz-laden room for the week. Anna was sitting on the bed with my purse in her lap. She looked odd. Her mouth was slightly open and she was moving her jaw from side to side. A small, staccato moan accompanied each swing of the jaw. It sounded like counting without the numbers. She was staring straight ahead, her gaze fixed in the distance, purposeful, but not for seeing. The rhythmic precision and dead-on concentration were familiar. When we were little, Anna used to curl up into a ball, her knees and arms and head tucked in as tight as she could, under her body. She would rock backward and forward in this position on her bed, butting her head up against the headboard. Not hard, really, just enough to make a sound, *clunk, clunk, clunk,* to accompany the same low, staccato moan, "uh, uh, uh." This was how she fell asleep every night. And this was *before* the lightning.

I suddenly recalled one night when my mother came into our room. I looked to be asleep but wasn't, and Anna was rocking and bumping and moaning. I am sure this wasn't the first time my mother had witnessed this, but it seemed in that moment to be a source of great sadness for her. She said, not so quietly, "Oh, Anna," as though Anna were engaged in something certain to cause someone great pain.

I had my back turned to Anna in her bed and my mother at the door. I was curled up and I was finishing a secret prayer. At the time, I kept a yarn-and-Popsicle-stick God's eye hanging in my window that I had made at my one week in Bible school. I sang the "Johnny Appleseed" prayer, silently, before dinner every night. I had been in Sunday school just long enough to know that noncompliance could get you in big, hellish trouble.

From this obedient position, I could hear my mother's footsteps as she walked to Anna's bed. I could hear it squeak once between the clunks and moans when she sat down. Anna kept on rocking. I thought my mother was probably rubbing her back, while she quietly whispered my sister's name. "Anna, Anna," she said in a hush, trying to capture her attention. Anna kept on rocking and banging her head and moaning. My mother whispered, "Anna, why do you do this?" Anna kept on. It was quiet for a while, except for the rhythm of the headboard bumps and my sister's moans. Usually, while Anna rocked, I counted. I remember being able to count really high, but Anna could rock even longer.

"Anna, please, can you tell me why you have to do this?" my mother asked again, quiet and pleading.

Anna kept on rocking and banging her head, but replaced

the grunting moans with words, spaced out to keep the tempo. "It . . . is . . . too . . . noisy . . . in . . . my . . . head."

"Oh, honey" was all my mother could say. After a few minutes, she got up and left the room, leaving Anna rocking and moaning and me secretly counting to keep track. I started over, silently, "One, two, three."

I came into my sister's grown-up guest room and sat next to her on the bed. I took my purse from her, but she kept on swinging her jaw and moaning, staring ahead. Her hands remained poised in the air, as though the purse were still perched between them. I looked in the direction of her gaze and saw us both, sitting on the edge of a twin bed, looking into the mirror on top of the dresser. I put my purse on the floor and took Anna's left hand in mine. I stared at us for a while, trying on swinging my jaw back and forth to Anna's pace. I used my free hand to pull my hair back, to see if we looked at all alike; sisters with ponytails making faces in the mirror. Somehow, without our knowledge or consent, we had left the forgiving place of youth and moved into a weary place of adulthood. While my sister tried to outwit the noise in her head, there was little else to do but count, only this time I counted aloud. "One, two, three, four, five, six, seven."

I got to ninety-seven and reached in my pocket for a cigarette, still counting, the ninety-eight and ninety-nine and one hundred muffled as I lit up and inhaled. One hundred one was followed by a huge sigh and smoke. This caught Anna's attention. I could see her eyes shift for a brief second toward mine in the mirror. Looking straight ahead, counting still, I handed the cigarette toward my sister. I watched as she swung her jaw to center, closed her mouth, and shut her eyes. She opened them a second later and took the cigarette. We remained on the bed, looking in the mirror. I stopped counting while she smoked. When she had smoked about half of the cigarette, she moved it back toward me, the ash long and menacing. I took it and tapped it into my hand. Anna put her hands in her lap and put her head down.

"I'm going to run to the store," I said, standing now and trying to figure out where to put the cigarette. I went to the window, opened the screen, and tossed it outside.

"Do you need anything?" I asked. Anna fell sideways, slowly, her upper body now on the bed but her feet still on the floor.

"Do you need anything from the store?" I asked again, as I picked up her feet and put them in bed with the rest of her. I stood there watching her for a minute, hoping she would respond to me. A single tear worked its way from her left eye down her cheek. She closed her eyes. I started to leave the room when I heard her say something.

"What?" I asked.

"I'm pregnant," she said miserably, her eyes closed. I didn't know what to say. I left the room and walked downstairs.

I drove out of the circular drive and back onto Maid Marian Way, past many large, imposing homes with subtle variations on the curious architectural theme of my sister's house, past the stone wall that announced the entryway to Sherwood Forest and back out into a world that felt somewhat familiar to me. I found a gas station with twenty-four-hour convenience store amenities and spent a considerable amount of time walking up and down the three short aisles. I tried to think about potato chips versus Fritos, Ding Dongs versus Ho Hos, double-A versus triple-A batteries. I tried to think about the cola wars. I remembered Chick O' Sticks and candy cigarettes. I bought three packs of Camel Lights, three cans of Tab, and mints. I stood outside the store and smoked a cigarette, taking deep, rejuvenating breaths of tar and nicotine to clear my head. And I thought about my sister.

Deep in the woods of Sherwood Forest, Anna's fairy tale was unraveling. I was less startled by my sister's unhappy announcement than from the tiny piece of evidence that the castle was beginning to flood again. And I wondered if she was trapped there, watching the water rise, too afraid to leave.

Swimming

Naked

28

I DROVE THROUGH the empty streets and felt like Dorothy trying to get home. I sang the foreboding, racing twister song in
my head as I accelerated through this tropical, art deco version
of Kansas, watching Cuban nightclub posters, a tiki torch, and
some humongous potted plants sail through the air. Not one
hit the car. I prayed I would make it to the hospital before the
cellar door was pulled shut.

The hospital parking lot was now almost completely empty.
I pulled into one of the reserved spots at the front of the
lot and ran inside through the driving rain. I was completely
soaked by the time I made it through the door to the ER. The
nurses looked up at me from their triage station. I leaned over,
out of breath, dripping water all over their linoleum floor.

"Can we help you?" one asked. I'm sure it was unclear to
them whether or not I had sustained some sort of injury in
the storm. It was a little unclear to me. My grasp of time and

events, the past and present, was becoming a bit imprecise. It was hard to believe that I had been awakened just this morning by Anna's caseworker, had then driven across the hot, flat state of Florida to stand in the rain with my father, and was now back, fresh from a trip to the store for hurricane supplies to say good-bye to my mother. My exhaustion was moving me into an unfamiliar state; I was acting on information coming from somewhere new to me. I could barely keep a thought in my brain. I was making decisions on impulses that emanated from somewhere else in my body, maybe my blood. It made my skin vibrate.

"No, thanks," I said to the nurse, heading off toward the elevator. I pushed the up button and stood there, trying to catch my breath, holding my plastic Wal-Mart bag against my chest. I turned around and looked at the door to the chapel. I had never noticed it was there before. I walked quickly back toward the ER nurses. They leaned back the slightest bit as I approached them. They had been trained to spot trauma, even the invisible kind. They knew precisely how a person might look as they came out of shock to discover deep and troubling wounds.

"I just need a towel," I told them. "I need to be dry."

They stood perfectly still, waiting for me to continue. I had not given them the information they required to know whether to simply take my pulse or to push the alarm for Code Blue.

"I want to go in there," I whispered, gesturing toward the chapel. I was preparing for a church experience with only a vague notion of how one might behave. I sensed that it would be good to be quiet and dry. "I don't have much time," I whispered, louder. "May I please have a towel!"

There was an odd sense of purpose coming over me and a plan was forming, only not the kind I was used to. My plans were linear and rational and bossy. This was a space without a shape. It was a voice without words. And it was soft. I was either going completely crazy or was divinely guided. I guessed that it must feel the same, insanity and epiphany, particularly for the godless. From the looks on the nurses' faces, it looked similar. One of them reached under the desk as though getting the loot to hand to the masked gunman. She handed me a towel, a small, silly towel.

"Thank you," I said as humbly as I could muster in my newfound state of piety/lunacy. I thought if this was grace it felt an awful lot like a panic attack. I wished for more drugs. I toweled off my hair and my face as I walked back to the chapel. I stood looking at the door and dried my arms. I stepped out of my mother's sandals and dried my feet. It seemed a Jesus-y thing to do. I stepped back into my shoes and pushed the door open. I was thrilled to find the chapel empty.

It was a small room, carpeted, with one central row of pews. I walked slowly past them, counting. There were ten rows in all. I walked sideways into the middle of the front pew and sat down. I put my bag of stars on the seat beside me and pulled down the bar in front of me. I knelt down and looked up at my surroundings. It took me a moment to get my bearings, visually. I blinked my heavy lids and attempted to clear my head. There was a Holy Koran and prayer rug in the left corner and a Bible and crucifix in the right. I had passed a menorah and Torah along the wall next to a lectern as I walked in. My memory of the specific death rites of each of these religions was now fuzzy. It had been less than a month since I was attempting to serve as my mother's nondenominational apostle. It seemed an eternity.

Straight ahead of me was a large stained-glass panel that served as the focal point of the chapel. I squinted to bring the picture into focus. When I realized it was the story of Noah's ark, depicted in red, green, yellow, blue, and brown pieces of glass, I felt something velvety deep inside me. The burning ache in my chest had been numbed. It was a Novocain borne of weariness, I supposed. I felt more exhaustion than inspiration.

I put my hands together and lowered my head in a prayer of sorts. The only words I could think of began to tumble around in my brain like the beginning of a nursery rhyme.

"When it storms they go two by two."

It was then I knew what to do. I stood up and left the chapel. I pushed the up button on the elevator, and waited to ascend. I waited to go lead my mother through the storm.

29

I OPENED MY eyes and felt a slow-growing sense of apprehension. I came to realize first and foremost I was horribly, intensely hungover. My head was pounding and my mouth was as dry as the state I was in, literally. I was still in Texas; I was pretty sure of that. In fact, it appeared I was in some seedy Texas hotel room. I was staring at a stucco wall painted burnt orange with a Tex-Mex faux-Kahlo print hanging crooked, as though someone had knocked into it. I suspected that there may be a sad and ugly story right there, in that crooked piece of bad art, featuring me. There were clues: the bedside table was host to an empty bottle of Jack Daniel's and an ashtray filled with the remains of small cigarlike cigarettes.

I turned my head slowly, out of both pain and fear, to look in the direction of the opposite side of the king-sized bed. There was definitely someone there. I could see brown curly hair and a naked back. This was cause for some concern as I had no idea where, precisely, I was or who I was with. At that very moment, the back and head moved and the body rolled over to face me. He was a man, just barely, more a boy. His chest was completely hairless and I wondered if he shaved at all. He opened his eyes.

"Hey there," he drawled. "How ya feelin'?" He stretched, lazily, as though he didn't have a care in the world.

I got up and yanked the green, flimsy blanket off the bed, clutching it with both of my arms to cover my naked self. I walked to the bathroom without saying a word to this southern stranger. I slammed the door and sat down on the toilet, still holding the blanket up around my chest. I peed forever, excreting all the alcohol and other yet unknown toxins that my organs were wisely rejecting. I was in such pain everywhere it was hard to focus on one smarting, throbbing, or burning thing over the other. But one thing did finally win out. In fact, as I came to consciousness sitting there staring at the occupancy regulations on the back of the bathroom door of the Austin Motel, I realized my back was killing me. I turned around to try to peer over my left shoulder and almost fell off the toilet. I was branded, like a fucking Texas cow. I had a goddamn tattoo. I had procured the first gnarled branches of my own lightning tree, inked into my flesh in the exact same spot where my father's had begun to crawl up his back. I slumped over, my head in my hands, and tried to massage some critical information back into my head.

I knew it must be Sunday. I had flown in from Cleveland on Friday afternoon. I had waited two hours in Houston to meet my mother's plane; she had flown in from Florida where she had just moved, freshly divorced from Red Dog. He had, apparently, frequently gone astray before running away for good. I watched her emerge from the gate into the airport. She put her hand over her eyes as though it was too bright in the terminal and peered left to right, looking for me. I hung back, leaning next to a pole across from her gate, and waited for her to find me. She looked tired and small. Her hair was pulled back in a loose ponytail and was naturally graying. She wore jeans and a red sweatshirt with some black pointy leather-like boots bunched around the ankles of her jeans. It was not a good look. She must have been dressing for Texas. I admit it was hard to know how to dress for rehab. In just four hours we were due for our Family Weekend orientation session at Sweet Home in Austin, Texas, where my sister had been admitted for her addiction to alcohol and painkillers twenty days earlier.

My mother's eyes met mine and she stopped, her head tilting to one side as she took me in. She smiled as though I was the person she most wanted to see in the whole world. She put her bulging, brown vinyl carry-on bag down beside her and opened her arms. I had no choice but to walk to her and into her arms. It was a made-for-television reunion and once we were actually touching each other, unable to see ourselves, too intimate for observation, it was clear that neither of us knew what to do. We patted each other—one, two, three—and then quickly disengaged. I grabbed her bag and began to move in the direction of the plane that would take us to Austin and to my sister.

STACY

SIMS

We walked quickly, both of us nervous about being on time. I had learned punctuality from my mother; only she had neglected to coach me on what might be expected of me upon arrival. I was always so focused on the getting there I never knew what to do once I had actually arrived. As the newly appointed curator of photography, I was now regularly invited to parties in art patrons' homes. I would arrive two minutes after the advertised time and would stand next to the buffet while the hostess put her earrings on and the caterers completed setting the table. I would watch the rest of the guests as they began to trickle in twenty minutes later, each with a warm greeting, a lovely wrapped gift, or a humorous anecdote regarding the drive over. I would head back to the bar, wink at the mustached bartender who had become my new best friend, and quickly down a shot of vodka. Soon enough, I would be chumming up to my fellow guests, making witty remarks and embracing one or two trustees a bit too tight, my breasts squished against their old man suits while their well-dressed wives looked on warily.

When my mother and I arrived at Sweet Home, precisely at 6:00 P.M. as requested, and saw Anna for the first time, we reenacted our version of the familial hug with her. I was pretty sure that Melissa Banks, the counselor, didn't have to hear a single word from any of us about how we interacted as a family after seeing us greet one another, then stand back and stare at our feet, without a thing to say. But that is precisely what we did for the next horrifying twenty-four hours; we attached words to our feelings and words to our thoughts and words to our history. We used more words about the inner workings of the Greene family than had ever or should ever have been spoken.

I got up from the toilet and shuffled the short distance to the tub. I turned on the water and pulled up the metal button for the shower. I stuck my hand in to adjust the temperature and wondered if it would hurt my tree tattoo even more than it did to be showered on. I closed my eyes and reached my hand behind my back and touched it. Oddly, it seemed to hurt more from the inside out than from the outside in. I decided I should face the water at all times, just in case. I stepped over the tub from the back and let the hot, pounding water punish me. I let it pelt me in the chest as I remembered the last two days.

When I first saw Anna on Friday night, I thought she looked good. I'm sure she would disagree, having been deprived of all her makeup, hair and nail tools, and selections from her vast, well-lit wardrobe. The last time I had visited her, a little over a year ago and precisely seven months before Maura was born, I had counted fifty-six pairs of shoes. Seven rows by eight columns of built-in cubbies, each filled with a pair of very expensive shoes. It was hard to imagine how she got them or where she wore them. The week I was there she never once left the house. She claimed it was because of her bad ankle.

We soon came to understand that this was part of her problem, a result of her "using." She was agoraphobic. At first I thought it was a good thing she was a rich alcoholic/

addict/agoraphobic. She simply paid "the help" to shop, cook, clean, run errands, and raise the girls. Then we came to learn this was just *another* part of the problem. All of these people, George in particular, had been enabling her. I wondered if the "real" Mexican gardener had any idea he was a codependent illegal alien.

Frankly, I liked this stripped-down, cleaned-up version of my sister. She had her hair pulled back in a pretty, loose ponytail. She wasn't wearing any makeup and was dressed in a pair of jeans and a plain white T-shirt. She looked tired and defeated, but she looked like a real person, a real sister. Her mask was gone. Apparently so were all of her other defenses. It is hard to imagine how a steady, and I mean steady, diet of Percodan, Darvocet, and wine can protect you from much of anything, but we learned it kept her far, far away from her feelings. And these people at Sweet Home were extremely interested in feelings. They were unnervingly, obsessively interested in feelings.

After we arrived, we went to dinner with Anna in the Sweet Home cafeteria. They tried to homey up the home but it reeked of institution through and through. The inquisition lighting; the slick, reflective surfaces; the bland, brown foods: it all spelled either hospital or jail. Anna was very demure. She reminded me of Anna after her monthlong sabbatical in her room. It was as though she had been taken into a witness protection program only they had neglected to tell her much about her new identity. So she spoke quietly, hesitantly, trying on a whole new outfit of words, a whole new wardrobe of feelings, and, apparently, a whole new suite of memories. She mainly picked at her food.

My mother was also unusually quiet. It was all very unsettling, sitting in this peculiar cafeteria with my addict sister and my nervous mother. I knew it was bad to wish for a drink but I most surely did. Thank God we were allowed to smoke. After we moved our brown food around and stammered out a few tidbits of pitiful conversation, we moved out to the terrace. We sat in silence, three on a match sitting on top of a picnic table, our feet planted side by side on the bench, overlooking a green field covered with a quilt of black-eyed Susans. I liked these famous Texas wildflowers. They reminded me of cheerleaders who smoked, the black eye the cigarette accentuating Susan's pleated skirt and pom-poms. I had read about the wildflowers on the short hop from Houston to Austin. I had actually been far more interested in another noteworthy Austin attraction: a huge colony of bats that lived under a bridge, flying out at night in one giant blanket of airborne rodents. That sounded like my kind of Texas fun.

Melissa called us inside. We followed her preppy, well-ironed, khaki-and-starched-blue self into a room that was such a cliché I laughed out loud: there were sixteen folding chairs set up in a circle in the middle of a nondescript classroom with white concrete walls, bare except for a "One Day at a Time!" poster, a dead cactus in one corner, and a black plastic garbage can in another. They were going to initiate us by bringing us all together, one big happy group of alcoholics and their fucked-up families.

We were instructed to introduce ourselves by our first names only, to share our relationship to the Sweet Home inmate, and to express how we were feeling. It was a horrible few minutes. The patients—Anna, Fred, Terry, and Jackie—were good at it. They had been doing this stupid "let's get to know our neighbors" routine for almost three weeks.

While watching my mother squirm uncomfortably in her chair as she looked at the floor and mumbled, "My name is Fay. I'm Anna's mother. I feel nervous," and seeing Anna's suspicious smile, I had a prescient vision of the hours to come. This was not going to be so much about Anna as it was going to be about us. And I had the creepy feeling that my mother was really going to get it. I felt raging anger, although when it came time to introduce myself I confessed only to feeling tired.

I sat waiting for the ambush over the next two long hours. It didn't come, not then. Instead, my mother and I and thirteen strangers learned more than we ever wanted to really know about my sister's descent into suburban hell, her own updated version of *Valley of the Dolls*. I knew she had been drinking since high school, but I had no idea how much. Nor did I have any idea that she had lost her virginity in the tenth grade, drunk, or that she only vaguely remembered telling the college-age boy, her friend's brother, to stop. The next thing she remembered was waking up on the couch in her best friend's basement, naked under a ratty blanket, a tiny trickle of dried blood between her legs.

I had no idea that since she married George she had been

drinking every single night, even when she was pregnant. She cried as she told that part of the story. Most everything else she said as though she were repeating someone else's sleazy tale, her eyes narrow, her brow creased as she tried to remember every repugnant detail. It didn't make me feel any better hearing how the others fell from grace: how Terry stole from her own children and prostituted herself for drugs; how Fred lost four jobs, two wives, and five children; and how Jackie had not come out of her house for three months, depending upon the kindness of a stranger who delivered ten party-sized bottles of cheap whiskey and a loaf of bread to her home each week. They could have told a hundred sad and compelling stories about their disease. It didn't make it any easier to hear what a miserable, sick life my sister had been leading.

"George shouldn't have been giving you the pills," I told her, one of my many attempts to blame him. In the vernacular of Sweet Home, we came to believe George had his own "issues." In fact, I spent a lot of time trying to divert Melissa Banks's attention from Anna's issues to George's *clearly* co-dependent behavior. He had thus far proved a handy decoy.

"That's not why I dropped her," Anna said, her cool, detached voice falling away to deep sobs. "She just fell out of my arms."

We all sat there in stunned silence. Something bad was going down. Anna had been talking about how she fell down and broke her ankle during a party, her Mexican party. My mother looked up at her, tears in her eyes. She had been staring at the floor the entire session.

Anna looked directly at my mother as she told the rest. She wiped her eyes and continued, her cold voice back with a hint of accusation thrown in. "I am here because I dropped Maura on her head in the bathroom. When I picked her back up I was standing in front of the mirror holding a baby I had just dropped on its head. I leaned over and locked the door to the bathroom and stood there, staring at myself in the mirror, watching the mascara run down my face as I cried, holding my screaming baby. I was drunk. It was ten in the morning."

"You didn't mean to," my mother said after a long and uncomfortable group silence, her first words since she had introduced herself.

"How would you know?" Anna accused, staring her down.

Somehow my mother had been demoted from hero to archenemy. Anna had just shoved her off the pedestal where she had been made to stand since I could remember. And the showdown had just begun.

30

I GOT OFF the elevator and ran down the hall toward my mother's room. I stopped short at the nurses' station. The wretched, pudgy, secret smoker nurse was pulling car keys from her giant handbag, making whining, complaining, and, most important, leaving sorts of sounds.

"You need to give Bella a ride home," I told her. She looked up at me. They all looked up at me, four nurses in all, frozen. They had the same scared look I had seen on the nurses in the emergency room. I didn't have time to dwell on it, their fear or what I might be doing to deserve such looks.

"Bella lives five minutes from here. Please take her home," I instructed. "I'll go get her." I walked toward my mother's room. I took a quick look back over my shoulder. Nurse Stupidhead was walking quickly toward the elevator.

"Do not move another inch!" I shouted, stomping my foot.

"Don't make me come get you," I added. She took another slow, small step toward the elevator.

"Goddamn it!" I said. I ran to her as she picked up speed toward the elevator. It was easy to catch her fat wobbly ass. I grabbed her arm and pulled her down the hall with me. One of the other nurses came toward us. She smiled. It was Eileen. She looked like a Nordic angel; her short white hair matched her uniform. She was the only one who had consistently been nice to me.

"Lucy, calm down. Let her go." She was standing in front of us with her hand out to block us like a traffic cop.

I grabbed the pager out of the pocket of my Wal-Mart sweater and threw it to her. She caught it neatly, snatching it with her traffic-stopping hand. I was impressed. But I was also very, very upset.

"Why did you call me? My mother is dying, right? I just need someone to take Bella home. She doesn't need to be here. She needs to be home," I ranted. They seemed to be listening, so I continued. Bella emerged from my mother's room and walked slowly toward us.

"Bella, I got all the things you wanted." I reached into my own purse and found my keys. I lobbed them over Eileen's head, never once letting go of my nurse hostage's arm. "This nice nurse"—I swung her toward me to see her name tag—"this nice nurse, Jenny McTavish, is going to take you home. Just get the stuff out of the car and go on home. I will stay with Mom." I had a hard time getting those last words out. I had reached the point below exhaustion and beyond anger and found sorrow waiting there. I was crying.

"I have the stars right here," I sobbed, shaking my plastic bag. I let go of Nurse McTavish's arm.

Eileen came toward me and put her arm around my shoulder. "I need to get Lucy settled in with her mother, but first we are going to sit down and have some juice." She led me toward a lonely chair behind the nurses' desk. I sat down and covered my face with my hands, pressing the top of the bag into my eyes.

"Jenny, please take Bella home. If you can't, find someone who will. Bella, have you said good-bye to Fay? You need to do that now, please." Eileen was like Noah, telling us how to pair up and what to do. I was happy to have her calling the shots. I peeled back the foil lid from the tiny plastic cup of orange juice she had given me. I drank greedily and handed her the empty cup like a toddler.

"Would you like more?" she asked. I nodded my head. "Would you like some cookies too?" I nodded again. I was desperate for someone to take care of me, even if it came in the form of being handed institutional snack foods.

"Your hair is wet," Eileen commented. "I don't want you to catch cold here at our hospital. Hang on a minute," she said as she disappeared into the room behind us.

The next thing I knew my head was covered in a clean, white towel, being massaged with her strong nurse's hands. I sniffled and hiccuped, eating a miniature chocolate chip cookie and drinking the startlingly cold juice. My head was rocking back and forth between her competent hands and the towel. I could smell detergent and cotton. I would have been happy to sit there forever.

My eyes were starting to close when I saw Bella walk out of my mother's room down the hall. She stopped outside the door and stared straight ahead at the wall in front of her. Just then, the lights flickered, going dim for a second then coming back even brighter. It felt like a flashbulb; it felt like another snapshot had been recorded for the record books. I wanted to keep this photo, not of Bella staring at the wall but the one of me being taken care of by someone.

"It's the generator," Eileen clarified. "We need to get moving, everyone." She put the towel around my neck and asked, "Lucy, are you ready?" like a salon assistant inquiring if I was ready to move to the stylist's chair for my haircut. She patted my shoulders and moved slowly down the hall, toward Bella. I stood up to follow her.

I looked over at Nurse McTavish and mumbled, "Sorry." She looked down at her feet in her own wordless version of an apology.

I walked up to Bella. She turned to me. She looked troubled; the creases on her face created a map of intense internal conflict. She sighed deeply.

"What?" I asked. "Is she . . . ?"

"No, honey, she's still with us."

"What then?" Bella was making me nervous.

"She is waiting for your sister," she confessed.

I gritted my teeth and wondered if I could keep the juice

Swimming

Naked

and cookie down. I looked at the floor and saw my bag of stars, clenched in my right hand.

"It'll be okay," I assured her. "You should go now. I'll come to your house when it . . . when she . . ."

She took me in her arms. I fell into her chest, allowing myself to take in all the skin and muscle and cloth and breath of a warm embrace.

"She might be waiting for your sister, but it's you she really needs," she whispered.

"I know," I whispered back.

31

I STEPPED OUT of the shower and dried myself off, careful to avoid touching my tattoo. I wrapped myself up in a towel and went out to properly greet Dan, the young man with whom I had had sex. My memory was still foggy but intact, for which I was only semi-thankful. My Sweet Home training had taught me that blackouts are a very bad thing, although this I had already suspected on my own. I always eventually remembered that which I did under the influence, for good or for bad, including last night's adventure. I had regained each and every sordid snapshot for my Texas scrapbook, including commandeering Dan at a country-western bar, insisting that I wanted to fuck a cowboy, get a tattoo, and see some bats.

I walked to the bed and sat down. Dan woke up and smiled at me.

"Are you a cowboy?" I asked.

"Nope. I'm a Sigma Alpha Epsilon, ma'am," he replied.

"Did you tell me last night that you were not a cowboy?" I asked.

"A few times," he said, pulling at the front of my towel. "How's your back? Let me see."

I got up and looked at him like he was way out of line. He looked back at me, bemused, and I remembered a couple of things we had done to each other just a few hours earlier. I turned around and lifted the towel to show him.

"It hurts," I confessed.

"Well, come here," he drawled; pretty sexy for a frat boy, I thought.

"I need coffee," I said as I picked up my clothes from around the room. I had a quick flash of pants and shirts and shoes being flung at the walls. I remembered standing under a bridge, Dan looking up under my Stanley Kowalski undershirt as I looked up to see the bats. I recalled his hunger and earnestness and the dimples that marked the spot right below where his wide, muscular back tapered to his amazingly narrow waist. I thought seriously about trying to fuck away my hangover rather than caffeinating it. Then I remembered the plane, my mother, Anna, and all the rest of it.

I got dressed and slid back the lock on the red metal door to Room 161 at the Austin Motel. Texas was the brightest place I had ever been, each day the sun coming up for a brand-new interrogation. I fished for my sunglasses and walked unsteadily down the sloping driveway toward the roadside coffee stand, mercifully located right next door to the motel.

I was trying to decide what, if anything, to put in Dan's

coffee when I glanced over at the last table under the hatched roof of this indoor/outdoor coffee shop. My mother was sitting there perfectly still, looking like she had been transported, taken up from her metal folding chair at Sweet Home. She had the same angry look on her face as she did when I left her there knee to knee with Anna.

Yesterday we had just finished our bland, brown lunch in the Sweet Home cafeteria when Melissa described how we would have an opportunity to speak to each other directly in the afternoon session, providing "a forum to let go of some deep emotional baggage you might be carrying around.

"This isn't just for your sister," she assured us. "It's for all of you. It's time to heal," she concluded, sagelike. I imagined her golfing on the weekends in smart, crisp shorts and a blinding white shirt, driving golf balls tremendous distances, fueled in part by excellent self-esteem, particularly after a tough week of good work in family healing.

I thought this sounded like a bad idea, this plan to agitate the past. I stirred more sugar into the terrible cafeteria coffee and watched the whirlpool in my Styrofoam cup. Somebody was going down today.

"Our secrets keep us sick," Anna had explained, staring at my mother, wearing a fake smile and employing her Mother fucking Teresa voice.

I felt sick myself. I could feel it coming. Anna totally had it in for my mother.

"This is going to be a private session, just the three of you," Melissa had offered, as though this would be a very comforting thing to know. "I will be there to facilitate, of course," she concluded, pushing her headband back one eighth of an inch then splaying her perfectly manicured fingers on the table to signal the end of the discussion.

My mother and I stared at her like we were totally dim-witted. Anna's smug smile was deconstructing into a twitch. Our family was built on secrets and whitewashed every year or so with a brand-new coat of denial. Melissa might as well have been describing just how short and pleasant a walk it was to meet up with the executioner.

"Ready?" she asked, her chair screeching its own vile warning as she pushed it back.

"I need to run outside a second," I said, desperate for a cigarette before we started this stupid, terrible session.

"Me too," chimed both my mother and Anna in unison. We had smiled at one another. It is good to have a bond, I thought, even if it is nicotine. Had we known Anna was such a big drinker, we probably would have made alcohol our family glue.

It seemed to work for most of the families I knew, particularly around the holidays. Someone generally got mad or hurt or sick or in trouble from imbibing too much of the alcoholic-bonding adhesive, but that would simply become fodder for next year's Thanksgiving or Christmas cocktail-hour story-telling. At my boss's house this past Thanksgiving I watched how it works. We moved quickly through the bottle of cele-bratory champagne, tossing back the cold, bubbly liquid like it was medicine, and then went for the serious stuff. As we sat around the den, eating shrimp and trying to make more liquid appear in our glass by rattling the ice cubes around, Patrick, the patriarch of this house as well as at the museum, began to tell the family stories.

Like when his wife, Dot, burned her hand taking out the turkey, having forgotten she needed an oven mitt. How they took the turkey and Dot to the hospital and the family ate in the ER waiting room while Dot was treated for second-degree burns on her hand. And how mad she was that they wouldn't give her any painkillers because she had had a drink or two. That was hysterical! The next funny, funny story was about the year their son, Jeff, now twenty-four and engaged to Carrie, a scotch-drinking Irish girl, brought home a tee-totaler from college. This girl, whose name no one could re-call (Amy? Ann? Andrea?), had been very uptight. According to Patrick she wouldn't even drink wine with dinner. She left the table before dessert was served and didn't come out of her room until morning, packed and ready to go. There were so many stories. We laughed until we cried and drank our drinks quickly, as though to replenish our tears.

Back at Sweet Home, as we were taking our final, lung-filling drags off our cigarettes, Anna turned to our mother. "Mom?" she said, addressing her in the pleading, plaintive way of children of all ages, as though we have just come to meet our real mothers after decades of searching.

My mother stared at the ground. She was no fool.

"Mom?" Anna repeated.

My mother finally looked up at her, squinting in the hard Texas sun.

"Never mind," Anna said, tossing her cigarette into a patch of black-eyed Susans. She spun on her heel and went inside. We followed her. We followed her sober, righteous self directly into the maelstrom.

There were rules. Melissa explained that communication was to be open and honest, but not judgmental. As my mother and Anna sat down to face each other, she instructed that everyone should state their feelings in the following way: "When you did thing X, I felt Y."

Within minutes I felt there seemed to be a fairly loose interpretation of the rules, particularly by Anna, who seemed to be just barely skirting around a statement that went something like: "When you fucked up every second of my childhood, I felt like having a drink and dropping my baby on its head."

Melissa seemed to be so enraptured with Anna's raw anger she didn't seem to notice my mother was about to be slaughtered in the process. I thought Melissa had some of her own issues. This cheerleader had a smoking gun.

I tried to interrupt, hoping a feeling statement would cut through Melissa's preorgasmic fascination with my sister's rage.

"I feel this cannot possibly be helpful for anyone," I tried.

"I'm sure this is calling up some things for you, Lucy. But please wait until your one-on-one session," Melissa reminded me, her voice cool cerulean, her eyes wild crimson. "Go on, Anna," she cooed, "you were saying . . . ?"

"Mom, I know this is hard for you, but I think it is important to my sobriety for me to say these things to you,"

Anna said, as though reciting her lines. "It's important for me to tell you how things made me feel." She stopped, her mouth puckering and unpuckering, her brow deeply creased. It looked like she was completely unsure of what to say. And it looked like she could not access them, these elusive feelings, no matter how hard she tried. My mother sat and stared at her, calm as could be. I wondered if she had been clever enough to medicate herself in some way. I stared at her huge, ugly purse and tried to figure out how to rummage through it without attracting unwanted attention as I sat there on the perimeter of the circle of death.

"Okay," Anna broke the silence, her voice like a bell.

"Okay, remember when you left me to take care of Lucy at the lake? And I had to stay with her when she had that terrible sunburn?" Anna interrogated.

"I vaguely remember that, yes, okay, I remember," my mother replied.

"Well, that made me feel like you were abandoning me." Anna slumped back in her chair and crossed her arms in front of her chest.

"Huh," my mother said.

"Huh," I thought, "I was the one with the fucking sunburn."

"When we went next door for dinner with the neighbors, you mean? And you and your sister stayed on the front porch? Then? That's when you felt abandoned?" my mother asked.

"It didn't matter where you went, it's just that you left. You always left," Anna said, starting to cry.

Swimming

Naked

"I didn't always leave, Anna," my mother told her. "I always stayed. For better or worse, I stayed."

"Yes, you did. Every time. You left us every time something bad happened," Anna sobbed.

My mother looked at Melissa, one eyebrow raised. It was clear she wanted some sort of explanation. I looked at her too. This was very confusing. It was as though Anna had lived with a different family, one where the mom left, not Dad and then James. We had plenty to deal with right here, in our family, the one I grew up in. She didn't need to go looking for trauma. I figured her alcoholism was practically handed to her on a platter the minute she saw Dad get struck by lightning. I was bewildered as to why we weren't hanging out in that memory territory.

"Remember, this is how Anna feels. She feels that you always left her alone when the going got a little tough," Melissa clarified. "Anna has spoken of this quite a bit in our sessions here. It is important to honor her feelings, even if you feel very differently."

"Okay," my mother said to Anna, "go on."

"Like when you made me stay in my room," Anna whispered. "And you didn't stop James from coming up there all the time."

"What in the world are you talking about, Anna?" my mother asked. "She wouldn't leave her room, no matter how hard we tried, and James practically saved her life," she said, turning first to Melissa and then to me. "What's this about James anyway?" she asked Anna angrily.

"He was always up in my room . . . doing . . . you know, stuff," Anna whimpered. "I don't want to say."

If this weren't so fucked-up it would have been downright fascinating. I wondered if Melissa had heard the word *delusional* at any point during her training. Anna's view of the world made mine seem utterly wholesome and compassionate, like I was Walker Evans alongside her Robert Mapplethorpe, both of us capturing completely different images of the same incidents for the family album. No wonder she was so afraid all of her life. She was totally warped.

"This is Anna's reality right now," Melissa explained to us. "This is how she feels."

"Would it help Anna to know that James was gay?" my mother offered, as though clearing up a little confusion over the time of day.

Anna wept harder, covering her head with her arms as though hiding from a huge blast of dynamite. Melissa stared straight ahead and took a deep breath. It was clear to me that at that precise moment, Melissa understood she was in way over her head. My mother sat up even taller in her chair, her shoulders back.

"James was gay, girls. I thought you would have figured that out by now. No offense, dear," my mother said, turning her direct, clear gaze toward Anna, "but he wasn't interested in you in *that* way. If you want to know the truth, he wasn't interested in me in *that* way. He was interested in some librarian named Bruce in Pittsburgh."

Melissa and I both stared at my mother, our mouths agape.

Anna continued to cry, her sobs getting louder and louder. I feared her peculiar history-filtering lens was at work, turning James into a very different sort of molester.

But she moved on. She left the James announcement untouched. She left this huge piece of previously unknown information to lie there, a new secret about a secret that we would never discuss again. Anna moved on to an incident about which she seemed particularly vexed. She was fixating on something my mother had done to her on one of our summer vacations, the vacation the summer before Dad got struck by lightning. She danced around this mystery incident like a stuttering viper, unable to spit out the real venom. I couldn't remember anything about the vacation she was talking about that seemed remotely memorable, except for losing Anna's suitcase and clothes on the way there. This, remarkably, she blamed on my father.

"You know what it was, Mother," Anna accused, drawing out the word *mother* like she was pulling taffy.

My mother stared at her, daring her to continue.

"Remember?" Anna prompted. "At the lake?"

"What are you talking about, honey?" my mother asked. I couldn't believe she could have an ounce of compassion left for my sister. She sounded exhausted and her eyes were flat, but the concern in her voice was evident. It rang through the room like a shotgun. It was weird, that it was my mother's voice cutting through the clutter of insanity, a buckshot of humanity.

"Okay," my sister warned, as though that was it, she was

about to tell the big ugly secret and that my mother had just asked for it.

"Remember when we went swimming naked?" she asked. Each word was slathered with innuendo of the worst possible kind, the implication more than I could bear. Not only had she just stolen my one fucking secret great thing and made it hers, she had ruined it.

My mother stared at her during the longest second of silence known to man, her face morphing from confusion to anger. Her eyes were no longer flat. As she slapped my sister square across the face, her eyes were their bluest blue, my mother a victorious beauty.

I didn't stick around to see how Melissa dealt with this more obvious infraction, this hitting business, or mine, the throwing of furniture. I took my folding chair and flung it back toward the wall and left Sweet Home. I left my mother, my sister, and Melissa to sort out the sad truth from some sordid distortion of the past. I took the rental car and drove straight to a bar, attempting to smash any remaining notions I might have had about our family history into tiny little wet and drunken pieces. I scattered the remains of my youth all around Texas, mainly in the kind of bars where disillusionment is worn as a badge of honor. I sprinkled the last of it under a bridge with a cowboy named Dan, who listened to me talk until I couldn't. I told him everything I could think to say about that which I could no longer be sure. Except for swimming in the lake with my mother. That was supposed to be mine and I was going to keep it that way. That and my tattoo.

Fuck my sister and her distorted memories. As they inked my flesh and I could no longer speak, Dan held my hand. He held my hand and watched them make a mark on me that no one could take away.

"Mom?" I called out softly, approaching her through a dappled path of sun, filtered through the thatched roof of the coffee stand. She looked up at me as though I were a stranger.

"Mom?" I repeated.

"Are you okay?" she asked, finally.

"I think so. Are you?"

She didn't answer. She picked up her coffee and her huge purse. She put on her sunglasses and turned to face me.

"Let's go," she said.

I said a fast good-bye to Dan and packed some toilet paper between my jeans and my tattoo as a pain buffer for the long trip home. I met my mother in the parking lot and we drove in silence to the Austin airport. We barely spoke on the plane to Houston. As I left her at her gate, she gave me a perfunctory hug and started to walk away. She turned back and looked at me.

"It wasn't great," she said. "But it wasn't that."

She was right. My sister, for whatever reason, had taken our sad truth and sullied it. But I couldn't say it. I couldn't exonerate her, my mother. Not then. Not there. I made a gesture with my arms, a silent question mark that said, "Who knows?" My mother stared at me with her piercing blue eyes, willing me to speak.

"Bye, Mom," I said. And I turned and walked away.

32

I ENTERED MY mother's room like a sullen teenager, dragging my feet so my sandals scraped against the linoleum tiles. Her room was glowing; the hanging television created a fluorescent shimmer, like she was being kept alive in the last viable cell of the ill-fated mother ship. I could hear the rain pelting the fortresslike glass of the hospital windows, beating out a rhythmic warning, accompanying a staccato beep from some monitoring device. It was a Philip Glass score for the end of my mother's life.

Kyle's tree photographs lined the barren room; twenty or so of them were taped to the white concrete-block walls at eye level, as though they were hung on an invisible rail. I started to take them down, starting with the one closest to the door, circumnavigating the room on a slow, circuitous course toward my mother's bed. There was one near-dead potted fern on the ledge by the window. I picked it up and dropped it into the wastebasket. It made a loud, hollow thump. I peeled the last photograph from the wall and stacked it with the rest on the table next to my mother's bed.

"What did you do with the trees?" she asked. I wasn't expecting her to speak.

"I couldn't see the forest," I responded, thinking I was remarkably clever for a girl with an acute case of metastasizing exhaustion and fear.

"I want to make something for you, Mom," I whispered, willing myself to continue.

I took the stars out of the Wal-Mart bag and tore the package open, peeling back the plastic window from the cardboard backing. They fell to the floor, at least a dozen stars scattered around the room, many of them under the bed.

"Crap, crap, crap," I mumbled. I dropped to my knees and began picking them up, putting them into the pocket of my cardigan. It had come in handy, I thought, this ugly Wal-Mart sweater. I picked up the last of the stars and stood up, coming up directly beside my mother's bed. It was the first time I had looked at her, really looked at her, since I entered the room. She smiled weakly, keeping her eyes closed, as though she knew I was looking at her. Maybe she was developing telepathic powers as she neared the end, as she started her journey into the great beyond, wherever in the hell that might be. I willed her to help me know what to do next. She was silent. As usual, I was on my own. I stuck with my own plan, as loosely formed as it was. I began to repeat a mantra to myself, "When it storms they go two by two, two by two, two by two."

"You'll have to excuse me, Mom," I said, flipping off my sandals and breaking my silent chant. I climbed up onto her hospital bed, grabbing onto monitors, IV stands, and other hospital paraphernalia to guide my way toward standing. I could just barely reach the ceiling. I removed the tiny pieces of paper that hid the gummy surface on the back of the stars. I stuck them here and there, creating my own fancy constellations on the ceiling above my mother's bed. I wanted stars everywhere. To adhere the last ten or so, I had to straddle my mother, one leg on each side of her emaciated frame. As I fished around in my pockets, feeling to see if I had any more stars, I looked down. She was staring up at me, her eyes wide open, as still as a corpse.

"Oh my God," I said, startled. She looked totally dead. "Mom?" I asked, hoping she would answer me, praying her last image on earth hadn't been of my crotch.

"What are you doing?" she asked. It was remarkable how much a dying person could sound just like my mother, full of suspicion and disdain to the bitter end.

I stepped over to one side of her and knelt down on the bed.

"Hi" was all I could think to say. I took the remote control from her bedside table. "I can't remember for certain," I told her, "but I am pretty sure that *The Tibetan Book of the Dead* does not recommend passing over to the other side while watching Jerry Springer."

"Where is Anna?" she mumbled. I turned off the television with a particularly aggressive click of the off button.

I turned myself around in my mother's bed so I could lie down next to her. I could see her looking over at me, distrustfully.

"Can you scoot over a tiny bit?" I asked. I wiggled myself into the small space next to her. It was terribly narrow and I was afraid that one of us would fall to the floor, so I turned over on my side. I rested my head in my hand and looked at her. She had squeezed her eyes shut like a small child who is afraid of the dark, like a little girl who would prefer to make up her own version of what happens when the lights go off than to see the real color of the night.

"Anna?" she asked.

"No, Mom," I whispered. "It's me, Lucy."

"Oh," she said. "Okay." She didn't sound disappointed, exactly. She sounded like she was trying to get clear on what was happening. That seemed fair.

"Mom, Anna can't come," I told her. I stretched out my right arm and lay my head down on top of it. I put my left hand on top of my mother's hands. She had them crossed on top of her chest. She was totally decked out for eternity. She had assumed the position. I squeezed her hands gently.

"Mom, Anna can't come because she's in rehab again. She actually wanted us to come out there. Both of us. For another round of family group therapy. Remember how much fun that was the first time? In Texas? I told her we were a little busy here in Florida, with you dying and all."

She didn't respond. I watched her chest slowly rising and

falling. I could hear what was left of her lungs rattling quietly as she took in her last breaths.

"She wanted to see you so much, Mom. But she's a mess. She has never gotten better. I actually think she has gotten worse since Texas," I said. "I know she loves you," I whispered, my voice catching.

I rolled over so I could look up at the ceiling. I freed my arm from where it was trapped behind my head and took my mother's hand in mine. We were squished in her hospital bed, lying side by side, holding hands. I laced my fingers through hers.

"Can you see the stars, Mom?" I asked. They were right above us, each a deathly greenish color, but a full field of glow-in-the-dark stars nonetheless. I peeked over to see if she was looking. She was. I started to talk, explaining what I saw in the constellations I had made, our family's astrological chart.

"Anna is in rehab and the photographs are by a guy named Kyle. He is a photographer, and yes, I slept with him, but only once and I think there might be something there, but he scares me. He seems so sure of himself, so sure of me." I wasn't certain but I thought I could feel her squeeze my hand, just a tiny little bit. So I continued.

"Oh my God, Mom. It has been really crazy. I went to see Dad. He is so pathetic. It started to storm and he looked up and told me he wasn't afraid. Christ. He was like a giant, hairy two-year-old. And Aunt Martha was as nice as can be, but that house . . . Have you seen it? I don't know if I would recommend a visit to Anna. Not unless she gets her act seriously together. Can you imagine? The cat hair alone could send the sanest person into a deep depression. Anna would stop at the first bar and drink everything in sight. Dad was working on some sad fount—"

My mother started to cough, a fairly hearty hack for a dying woman. I was reminded that this was probably not the time for me to prattle on ad nauseum, although I was remarkably comforted by this new mother/daughter relationship. I suddenly wished I had been the kind of daughter who not only spoke to my mother about life's mundane details but touched her as well. This had been Anna's role. Up until Texas, anyway. She had always taken up so much of my mother's space, I just figured there wasn't any left for me. And once that distance was set in my mind, there was no way in hell that I would have traveled it. I would rather have walked through fire than to give my mother an emotional or physical inch.

Until now. Now I wanted to wrap my arms around her and hold on to her like Anna used to do. I wanted to climb inside of her and find the comfort that children believe only their mothers have to give. I wanted to get what I hadn't gotten. I wanted to fill up the space inside of me that ached for all the wrong things. I wanted to start over. I wanted to be a different sort of daughter. I wanted to be my sister, who had begged for my mother's love without shame. I wanted to change all of the family photographs, the real ones and the ones in my head. I wanted the seminal image to show two girls attached to their mother, both of us wrapped around her waist, looking up at her adoringly.

Then I remembered the problem. I saw the new revisionist photograph. There we would be, Anna and me, two members in the cult of my mother, beseeching her for her love. And there she would be, looking off into the distance, her blue eyes seeking her own unrequited love, her own missing affection. She had what we wanted, what we needed. She had revealed it to us at the lake, a glimmer of how she wanted to be. She wished to be a different kind of mother. She wished to be the kind of mother who goes skinny-dipping with her daughter and weaves fables from the stars and carries her home and tucks her into a feathery bed and then sits by her side, petting her hair, smoothing it down her back until that little girl falls asleep, knowing without a doubt that she is deeply loved.

Both my sister and I had misunderstood. It was too intimate for Anna, and I thought it had been a promise for more. But it was what it was. For me, it was one pure moment in time when the stars aligned so that my mother was overflowing with grace, so much so that she could bathe me in it. It just felt like the water from the lake on my skin. It just looked like the stars. It was, in fact, my mother's finest moment.

So I told her that. I held her hand and we looked up at the stars. I called up every single detail for her, from my sweat-drenched T-shirt to her beautiful, long, swinging hair to the sensation of the water on my naked skin, soft and slippery and dangerous and good.

I turned to face her and moved down the bed so I could put my arms around her waist. I curled up next to her with my head on her belly and held her like I wished to be held. I told her I loved her. I stayed right there, listening to the rain's steady beat on the windows and her raspy, tired breath. I could feel her heart beating. I wished I had held her like this a million times. I began to cry into her stomach. It was as much for being lucky enough to hold her this way just once as it was for the sadness of never having done it before. I held her tight and cried the tears I had been storing up my whole life. I let them wash over her body, preparing her in the only way I could think to: I anointed my mother with my secret love for her.

When I felt her heart stop I imagined her swimming toward the brightest star in the sky. When I didn't hear her labored breathing anymore I saw her dive under the water. She came up once and looked back at me, her blue eyes gleaming under the light of the stars. She smiled at me and then she dove back under the water. I didn't see her come up again. But I waited for a long time. I waited until morning, lying there with my arms around her, until the storm had passed and the sun had come up.

It was then that I finally let my mother go, swimming naked into the unknowable, enigmatic to the end.

STACY

SIMS

33

THE PORCH DOOR slammed and scared the crap out of me. I threw my cigarette deep into the woods and began to walk toward the house as though just returning from a leisurely nighttime stroll. My sister was backlit by the bright light from the porch. I watched her pull a single cigarette out of the pocket of her shirt, one of George's tattered, old dress shirts. She looked around to see if anyone was looking and lit up. I stepped behind a tree and stayed there out of her line of sight to let her smoke her cigarette in peace.

We had been at the lake for four days, just me and Anna and the girls. We were just starting to feel something that resembled comfort with one another. This feeling of double sibling harmony was seriously helped along after I drove an hour to a real town to rent a fucking VCR and twenty videos for the girls. They were the most annoying young women I had ever met, Sarah more than Maura. They were hostile and cold and humorless, particularly to Anna.

"Nice hat, Mother," Sarah would say, looking down her perfect, thin nose at us before strutting toward the pebble beach like a runway model, wearing a minuscule bikini over her emaciated eleven-year-old frame. Her eating disorder was rivaled only by her anger. She was really, really angry. Maura tried desperately to be as mad as her older sister. The most animosity she could muster was to confirm Sarah's cruel remarks to her mother with a "yeah!" At first I wondered if she was a little moronic, having been dropped on her head and all. But as her sister would swagger off without a second thought, Maura would always turn back, mortified, her face screaming a silent "sorry!" toward Anna. She wasn't incompetent. Instead, she appeared to have a sliver of compassion left for her recovering mother.

Anna had been sober exactly one year and twenty days, twenty days longer than my mother had been dead. We were here at the lake in Canada to deal with my mother's remains. And my sister's too. This was the longest she had ever been sober since she was fifteen, or so she claimed. She seemed to be made up of a thin veneer of eggshell and raw nerves. She would be fine one minute, funny even. I would be laughing at one of her self-deprecating remarks and would turn around to find her crying. She had left the house each day in search of an AA meeting. She returned the second day after just a few minutes and practically fell from the car, shaking from head to foot and sobbing. She was inconsolable for hours. The girls just rolled their eyes and went to the beach. I stayed with her in her room, rubbing her back. I even tried counting. When I asked her what was wrong she said, "I am profoundly sad, all the time."

So considering all of that, I gave her a break on the smoking. It was easy, as I was also still smoking. I had, in fact, cut way, way down. I sometimes smoked less than ten cigarettes a day. But it was hard. It was especially hard as this was the night we intended to dump our mother's ashes in the lake. I suppose when the time came we wouldn't actually just dump Mother's remains. We would waft, sprinkle, or spread them somehow. We would let the breeze take them and send them flying over the lake. The girls would stand there with their arms crossed and look disgusted. They would ask, "Can we go now?" Anna would probably start trembling and rub her neck so vigorously I would think she was having breathing problems. She had explained that this is where it hurts her. This was where she physically felt the pain of withdrawal and yearning. This was where she burned for another drink. I knew the pain myself. Oddly, smoking relieved it; the hot smoke somehow soothed the searing pain in my throat.

If I could have delayed our sure-to-be-touching memorial service for my mother, I would have. But both George and Kyle were due tomorrow. It was going to be weird enough with all of us at the house together; Kyle had been silently interrogating me with his solid, spooky, loving ways since I had come home from Florida. Everyone I knew had taken to calling ours a "healthy relationship," which, while incredibly annoying, seemed like it might be true. But I was still a nervous wreck. As were both George and Anna, apparently. With Anna newly sober, they were like newlyweds with skid-row baggage.

I peeked out from behind my tree to see if Anna was done with her cigarette. She took a final, throat-medicating drag and flicked it into the woods. I coughed to announce my presence then began to head toward my sister.

"Hey," I called out.

"Hey," she said back.

"So, I guess we should do this thing," I said, as enthusiastically as I could muster.

"I'll have to tear the girls away from *Dirty Dancing*," Anna said. "They have watched it five times already today. I think they want this vacation to be like that movie. They have a totally warped, romantic view of the world," Anna mused, shaking her head.

"I don't know where they get that from," I said, sarcastically.

"Me either," Anna replied, earnestly.

"I'll get them," I said, jogging up the wooden steps. "Need anything?" I asked.

"A beach martini and . . . ," Anna began. I stopped at the door and spun around. "Kidding," she said, looking down at her grass-stained sneakers.

The girls were as close to the television as you could get and still have a sense of anything beyond brightly colored pixels.

"He is so hot," Sarah was saying to her sister.

"Yeah," replied Maura. "Hi," she said to me. I was beginning to like her just a little bit. Sarah gave me a shitty, insincere smile.

"Young ladies, it is time to bury your grandmother," I announced. "Now where did I put her?" They stared at me in horror as I looked under the couch, behind the chair, and in the junk drawer. I started dancing along seductively to "Baby" as I continued to pretend to look for the box filled with my mother's ashes. It was so easy to appall them. They had led a very protected life. While my sister secretly fell apart she insisted that everyone, herself included, upheld an odd set of old-fashioned manners and rules that she had lifted from romance novels.

"Fuck, where is it?" I asked, throwing my hands up and looking to them for guidance.

"You're not allowed to say that," Maura told me.

"No, *you* aren't allowed to say that," I told her. "I'm allowed to say it all I want."

I was not the model aunt. I was an aunt modeled after the aunts I had known. I took Martha's eccentricities and mixed it with Sally's sense of humor and threw in my own foul mouth for good measure. I had, in fact, invited both of the aunts to come for this odd gathering here at the lake. Martha sent a nice note declining and asked me to send pictures from the vacation for Dad. Sally was still stationed in Burma with the Peace Corps and could no more easily get home now than she could when my mother was sick. She wanted pictures too. I hoped Kyle could shoot more than trees.

"Here it is," I said dramatically, lifting the metal box out of its cardboard packing box. I had left it on a chair in the dining room. The girls continued to stare at me, kneeling up to look over the television set, keeping an eye on my every move.

"You guys," I said, as kindly as I could muster. "This is going to be hard on your mother, so please be nice." Sarah made a sound of disgust and rolled her eyes. Maura stared at the box in my hands. "Okay, if you can't be nice just please be quiet," I pleaded. "It won't take long," I promised. "We aren't exactly experts at this sort of thing so there is only so much we can make up to do."

"Can I hold it?" Maura asked. Sarah swung her head around to stare at her, *Exorcist*-style.

"Okay," I said, handing it to her. "Do you want to carry it down to the lake?" I asked her.

"Yes," she replied. She should try out for the color guard at school, if they still had such a thing. She held that box like a soldier with the American flag. I gave her sister a look. I intended to convey, "If you say one fucking word I will wring your neck." Apparently, she got the message.

We walked down to the pebble beach single file. We didn't utter a word. Maura led us, walking excruciatingly slowly, carrying her grandmother's ashes. Her sister followed, picking up stones along the way and whipping them into the woods with surprising strength. It was pure anger; she had no muscles. Anna walked behind her daughters, one hand to her throat, the other clenching her shirt, holding it tight against her chest. I followed the three of them. I closed my eyes and tried to walk a few steps at a time in total darkness, in honor of my mother and my memory of the time she took me swimming here at night, a million years ago.

When we got to the edge of the water, we lined up along the shore. The water was almost completely still. There were nearly imperceptible waves pushing at our toes. I kicked my sandals off. Anna and the girls stared out at the water, frozen. I stepped into the water so it covered my feet. It was as warm as my skin and felt heavenly. I unzipped my shorts and let them drop by my feet. I stepped out of them. I took off my T-shirt. I was wearing a bathing suit. I stepped into the water a little farther and turned to face my sister and her daughters and smiled. I knew what to do. I took off my suit and tossed it over their heads onto the beach.

Anna closed her eyes and shook her head. The girls stared at me, horror-stricken.

"I don't know if your mom ever told you," I said, "but we have a family tradition here at the lake. Your grandmother started it. Can I have the box?"

Maura handed me the box. She looked me directly in the eyes, terrified to look down. I looked directly at her as I continued.

"Your grandma took both your mother and I skinny-dipping at night when we were little, younger than you girls," I explained. "So I'm going to take her ashes out into the lake in my birthday suit. Care to join me?" I turned my gaze to my sister. "Anna?" I asked.

"Well, all right then," I said, turning to wade deeper into the lake, giving my sister and her daughters their first full view of my tattoo. I had never told Anna about it. And I was certain that Sarah and Maura knew nothing of their grandfather. We weren't that kind of family. We told no tales. Especially not that one.

"Oh, for God's sake, Lucy," Anna cried out as Sarah and Maura gasped in unison.

"What is that?" Sarah asked, trying hard not to sound too intrigued. I knew I had just become extremely interesting to her.

"Come on in and I'll tell you," I called back.

"But we don't have our suits," she whined.

"I know," I countered. "Come on, you chickens!"

I kept walking, moving slowly into the lake. I held the box up high over my head. I looked back over my shoulder once. All three of them were standing perfectly still, staring at me. I turned back around and kept wading deeper and deeper. I was almost to my neck, the water now covering my tattoo when I heard the splashing sound of someone running into the water. I turned around and saw my beautiful, strange sister dive naked into the lake. She began to swim, a slow crawl, as though this was the most easy, natural thing in the world.

"Mom!" the girls screamed, both excited and mortified.

"Come on," Anna shouted back to them, swimming up beside me. "Jesus, Lucy," she said. "You know they probably think you're some sort of freakish, tattooed lesbian now," she scolded.

"You have some odd ideas about things, dear sister," I replied. "Besides, they won't think anything of the sort when I tell them how many men I've slept with," I whispered. "Come on, you little chicken shits!" I yelled.

"Aunt Lucy!" they shouted, this time with more affection than disdain. I looked back and was elated to see them wriggling out of their shorts and T-shirts, giggling madly. They ran at full speed, their arms crossed over their nonexistent breasts, until they crashed into the water. They swam out to us. We had moved far enough into the lake where we could barely keep our heads above water, where it was too deep for the girls to stand. They each wrapped an arm around their mother's neck to keep them afloat. I looked at Anna and saw tears in her eyes. I suspected it was a long time since her daughters had touched her in any way.

"Should we say good-bye to your grandmother, girls?" I asked.

"Yes," they said, through chattering teeth.

I reached up and opened the box. I held it in both hands and began to swing it around my head, turning slowly in the water, letting our mother's ashes fly in a circle around us. The night was still, so the dust began to settle, surrounding us like a ring of fairy dust. Maura reached over and put her arms around my neck, letting her body rest against my back. Sarah attached herself to her mother in the same way. We floated out there for a long time looking at the sky, at the stars, and at the undulating ring of ashes around us. Then we swam through them, letting the ashes glaze our naked bodies as we headed back to shore, two by two.

Acknowledgments

I AM FOREVER grateful to *Swimming Naked*'s first reader, Jay Bolotin, and to early readers Aralee Strange, Markus Trice, Rosemary Seidner, and Elizabeth Logan Harris. I am especially thankful to Susan Andrews Grace, who convinced me I was on the right track. I look forward to meeting Susan in person!

I am also thankful to Sally Lachina for sharing with me her own story of when she recognized the secret person inside her mother and to the Tuesday Morning Women for teaching me every important thing I know.

I am tremendously lucky to have Deborah Schneider as my agent and friend. I think it is beyond luck that I came to have Molly Stern as my editor. I am deeply moved by the circumstances of our working relationship and our growing friendship.

I am profoundly blessed by my family and friends, and I hope most of all to impress my son, the inimitable Nick Sharp. Thank you, everyone.